ANGER THROWS A CURVEBALL

ANGER

THROWS A CURVEBALL

Paul Venosdel

SMB
Sunrise Mountain Books
Boise, Idaho

ANGER THROWS A CURVEBALL
"Baseball with an Attitude"-Book One

ISBN 978-1-940728-07-0

2016 First Edition

Published by Sunrise Mountain Books
13347 W. Tapatio Drive
Boise, ID 83713
www.sunrisemountainbooks.com

Printed in the United States of America

Dedication

This book is dedicated to
my friend, soulmate, and wife, Cindy,
and our two boys, J.D. and Brett.

Cindy is a special, loving, human being, and I am grateful to have her in my life. She has supported the boys and me through our journey into the chaotic youth baseball underground, which takes up more life than anyone can imagine. She is an incredible scorekeeper, great encourager, and fierce protector of all her boys. Look out when one of her sons is on the pitcher's mound, as her pacing may make you seasick! Eating dinner at 9 p.m., six days a week for six to eight months, is not an easy lifestyle to sign up for. And no one signs up for youth baseball with a love of scrubbing baseball pants at 11:00 at night to get laundry completed for the next day's games. She travels long distances with overnight stays in remote towns across the Mountain and Pacific Time zones to support her boys. Taking time away from her work is difficult, but a labor of love.

I am blessed beyond belief to have two boys who love the game of baseball and who have allowed me to coach their teams. As the coach's sons, J.D. and Brett are under tremendous pressure from teammates, coaches, and parents to produce unparalleled results on each and every play during baseball games and practice. The boys are required to get to practice early and stay late after practice, which adds stress to studying for exams and getting homework completed on time. The boys help set up stations, prepare the field, and load up the truck with equipment. J.D. and Brett are two very special young men.

Acknowledgments

I can't thank enough all the players and parents I've had the privilege to be around during each baseball season. Good and bad, the players and parents have taught me a lesson about life and baseball.

It's with special appreciation to my parents, Dan and Helen, and my brother, Eric, whose continued love and support inspired this book. My parents raised me in a sports world and I'm thankful to have their support. Youth baseball has changed since I played; however, they instilled values that still hold true today. Special appreciation to my brother Eric for his support and encouragement, too. He is blessed to have two wonderful girls and is living vicariously through his two nephews who love baseball. That is a special treat to share.

I am especially grateful to have shared a baseball dugout with the following amazing individuals who have brought a special youth baseball experience to my life: Jeff Likes, Terry Fesler, Jason Robarge, Fred Anzaldua, Brad Schmidt, Craig Pulley, and Mike Thiry.

I miss Ruth Knoblock. Her inspiration to write this book lives on today. Marilee Donivan is a gift from heaven.

And without Jesus Christ leading this journey, there would be no peace, no joy, and no Victory!

Contents

Foreword i

CHAPTER 1 ....**19**

The Car Ride ....

CHAPTER 2 ....**33**

Yes, We Are Talking About Practice.....................................

CHAPTER 3 ....**56**

Stats, Stats—Everywhere Stats..

CHAPTER 4 ....**68**

The Line Up Card ....

CHAPTER 5 ....**88**

Sellout Crowd..

CHAPTER 6 .... **106**

Under the Lights...

CHAPTER 7 177

    Instant Replay ....

CHAPTER 8 185

    Scoreboard...

POSTSCRIPT 200

    Player's Code of Conduct Pledge 201

    Parents/Managers Code of Conduct Pledge 203

ABOUT THE AUTHOR 205

Foreword

This book is realistic fiction. The names of the players and coaches are made up. I did, however, make my son cry during 8-year-old baseball. I have yelled at him on car rides home from the fields. I have felt the wrath of youth baseball parents. Our teams have been in closely-fought baseball games, and I've lived and died on every pitch my sons have thrown and every at bat they have taken.

Flashback: In the hospital while my wife endures 23 hours of labor with our first son, like most dads, I think about what his life will be like with him in the world. Will he want to play sports? Throw a football or hit a baseball? Shoot hoops? Will he want his dad to manage his team? Will my son prefer to play a musical instrument in the band?

At a very early point in their childhood, both my sons took to throwing and catching a ball. God blessed my sons with athletic gifts and talents. They have a love of competition and enjoy playing sports with friends.

Anger Throws a Curveball is a reflection point for the last eight years of being involved with my son's baseball teams. The book tells a story about a twelve-year-old boy and his teammates. What started out as unbridled joy and excitement to be around youth baseball has brought a pause to see the game through the eyes of children.

Quoting lines from movies for everyday life references is as American as apple pie, ice cream and baseball. Tom Hanks famous line in the 1992 movie a League of Their Own, "Crying? Crying? Are you crying? THERE'S NO CRYING IN BASEBALL!" is a line I have used and thought of when I see young ballplayers crying on the field. Over the last couple of seasons watching the Little League World Series on television and witnessing crying on the field in six different states of games my sons have played on it's time for a national discussion on crying in youth baseball.

Failing to live up to coaches' and parents' unrealistic performance standards yields anger from the youth ball player resulting in a release of emotions in the form of tears. There is an answer, however, to beating this anger.

There is obviously room for crying in baseball when an injury happens on the field. There is no room for crying when fans, parents and coaches yell and scream at a ball player that results in tears. There is no room for crying in baseball when a ballplayer puts so much pressure on himself to deliver positive results that a failure should bring an overwhelming flow of tears streaming down his face.

Not every parent, child, and coach behaves poorly in every youth baseball game. Not every parent, child, and coach yells and screams in youth baseball. Not every child cries because they fail to make a proper play or can't control their emotions playing the game of baseball.

I understand the viewpoint that America is an outraged, narcissistic, social media-driven society with helicopter parents, daddy-ball coaches, one sport only focused kids, common core standards, measuring how you feel about an answer more than what the answer is and success is measured by how many possessions you own.

Managing 23 youth baseball teams, I've seen the desire kids have to please their parents, family, friends, coaches, and teammates up close and personal. When kids don't live up to the tremendous amount of pressure they put on themselves and feel from the outside, their only reaction to get the failure out of their minds is overwhelming disappointment, anger, hatred, and the simplest release of emotions is crying. When the emotional dam breaks, the tears are uncontrollable.

Managing teams with players ages 6 to 14 comprised of roughly 500 parents wanting their son to start at shortstop and pitch every inning while batting first in the batting order, I've had the unique position to see the desire of loving parents who lose a sense of reality and demand that their child perform at a major league baseball talent level. Pressure—to field every ground ball and fly ball, hit every pitch, and never make an out—results in crying when they don't live up to their parent's standards. Fake praise from parents causes the same feelings of rejection in their children and also brings forth tears on the baseball field. Youth baseball parents' main desire is to have their children start on the high school varsity baseball team, be offered a Division One college scholarship, and/or be drafted onto a major league baseball team.

Managing roughly 375 youth baseball games against other youth baseball coaches, I've experienced their desire on and off the field to be the best, relive glory days gone by, and scream at underperforming players, resulting in crying from young children.

This book would not have been written if it had not been for the grace to be able to manage youth baseball teams. I have enjoyed coaching, and the experience to be around a great group of players, parents, and coaches. No doubt, I've enjoyed winning more than sixty percent of games coached, along with the twelve league tournament championships. Watching my son shine on the baseball field and teaching young players to respect the great game of baseball is truly rewarding. Wins and losses do fade away and championship trophies will end up in a box when the boys leave the house, but speaking truth into children will hopefully last a lifetime.

Chapter 1

The Car Ride

"Now batting for the Los Angeles Dodgers, start-ing at the catcher position and wearing number 1 on his royal blue uniform! Brent Ryan!" The loud speakers at Dodger Stadium ring out with the sweet sound of *"Brent, Brent, Brent! Ryan, Ryan, Ryan!"* –the chant echoing throughout the sellout crowd of 56,000 fans. The patrons go crazy as Brent walks toward the batter's box with the baseball game on the line.

The Bermuda grass throughout the outfield has a special shine and smell that is mesmerizing. The casual baseball fan sitting in the bleachers sees infield dirt, but the professional baseball player smells a perfect combination of diamond dust and red clay mud evenly distributed between the infield and outfield grass.

The sky is clear and the weather is a calm 70 degrees. With his right foot in the back of the batter's box and his right hand held up high in the air to the home plate umpire, he is requesting time before he's ready to hit. Brent bangs his 36-inch 30-ounce cupped wooden Louisville Slugger bat against his blue metal spikes. He tightens the velcro on his batting gloves, straightens his pine tar stained helmet on his head, and digs in, ready for a 100-mile per hour fastball from the San Diego Padres relief pitcher.

He can barely focus as the stadium cheers thunder around him as if he were standing in front of a 747 jumbo jet airliner ready for takeoff down the runway! The Dodger Blue faithful fans stand up from their seats and begin to scream their heads off as they encourage their hero to deliver the game-winning walk-off hit.

Man, what a moment! What a game! A lifetime dream coming true—right in front of Brent's eyes.

"Brent. Brent! Hey, Son, are you listening to me? What on earth were you thinking? You lost the regular season game to the Westside Warriors! Really, because you didn't swing at that pitch? There goes *OUR* perfect season and undefeated record. I hope you're happy!" The voices of Brent's parents are thundering from the front seat of the family truck.

Pablo and Kay, Brent's parents, are more frustrated with the feeling that *they* lost the game and *their* son didn't deliver the game-winning hit to keep the regular season winning streak alive. Kay is still furious that Kylan— *Kylan,* of all kids—struck out Brent to end their undefeated regular season.

Deep down, Kay is seething, knowing that when she sees Kylan's mom Bernice around their small town in Idaho, the talk for the next *thousand* years will be about how Kylan struck out Brent! Kay won't be able to go to the WinCo supermarket or library without being confronted with the failure of her family. Brent's mom Kay, and Kylan's mom Bernice have their own bad blood rivalry, dating back to when their boys attended pre-school and play group together.

21

Meanwhile, the car ride home in the winning pitcher's red Dodge minivan isn't much better for Kylan. Kylan's mom doesn't let the fact *he* walked a batter and hit a batter in the game vs. rival Eastside Eagles escape the winning celebratory mood. "You are so lucky, Mister, you won that game. Your curveball was flat, and you had nothing on your fastball. See what happens when you don't eat all your breakfast! I told you to go to bed at 8:30 last night. You looked so tired!" Bernice bellows.

Kylan is also reminded a hundred times about the money and time Bernice has shelled out to his private pitching coach—a former single A thrower who spent time in the minor leagues with the Hillsboro Hops and Helena Brewers. And how they are all disappointed he won't focus more on his pitching mechanics.

"Kylan! Kylan! Are you listening to me?" hisses Bernice. Kylan drifts off into dreaming about the baseball game just played and how fun it will be to someday get interviewed on ESPN like a major league baseball All-Star.

Brent lives in the Eastside Little League Eagles' district boundary. Kylan lives in the Westside Little League Warriors' boundary.

No doubt about it, Brent struck out, to end the team's perfect season. There's still a chance to win the league playoffs, but the undefeated season is history. Brent couldn't control his emotions, and his anger let loose crocodile-sized tears on the baseball field. Brent will look back some day at the video his family shot of this baseball game and see a waterfall of tears that would rival Old Faithful in Yellowstone National Park.

All the yelling, all the screaming, the hours of hard work at practice, his parents, his coaches, his teammates, the chance for perfection are now gone like the baseball game itself. Brent's furious anger and utter failure to perform with the game on the line needed some place to go. It took the form of big salty tears streaming down his eye-blackened cheeks.

Lost in the car rides of both boys' families' "what if" replay diatribe regarding the regular season game is the fact that Westside and Eastside are the two best teams. They will meet again in the Little League Championship game. The regular season matchup between Eastside and Westside was thrilling. The Little League Championship game rematch will be fantastic.

What a game the two best teams just played, featuring *the* best 12-year-olds in the Treasure Valley of Idaho! The boys on both teams played a hard-fought game with tons of action and an incredible ending. And they get to do it all over again in a couple of weeks.

The Eastside Little League Eagles and the Westside Little League Warriors have an intense rivalry that surpasses USC vs. UCLA, Michigan vs. Ohio State and Duke vs. North Carolina, all combined. Over the last three seasons, Eastside and Westside have played for the Idaho Little League Baseball State Championship. The intense rivalry between the two teams did not stop them from engaging in the time-honored tradition of the end-of-game sportsmanship handshakes after their well-played baseball game.

As is the custom after a Little League baseball contest, each team forms a line at home plate to fist bump each other and utter a fake and slightly audible "good game" groan. The joyous Warriors and distraught Eagles saunter through the line like zombies with their heads down, and right fist in a ball, bouncing off each other mumbling "Good game" fifteen times, 12 players and 3 coaches to each line.

For Eastside Little League—and Brent, especially—the postgame ritual of shaking hands with the opposing team after the loss is like driving a car through thick fog.

As if the postgame handshake fist bump fiasco isn't enough torture, Brent must get prepared for the other youth sports tradition—the postgame talk by all the coaches. Upon the completion of each and every game, Eastside coaches insist on talking with the team in the outfield, away from any spectators and parents.

The experience this time is especially mind-numbing as the coaches' yelling seems to take weeks to complete. Brent and his Eagles teammates faintly hear something about needing to have fun when you play, come out ready to battle from the first pitch. However, to the 12-year-old boys from the Eastside Little League, it sounds like Charlie Brown's teacher in the Peanuts holiday cartoons on television.

The Eagles coaches finally complete their postgame gum-smacking session. After round and round discussions on the team's fielding errors, missed chances at the plate to hit the baseball, and lack of killer winning attitude, the sound waves finally subside.

Eastside players leave the outfield grass, and stroll slowly back to the dugout to divvy up carrying the team gear to Coach Pablo's truck. The team gear bag is full of baseballs, catcher's gear, and batting helmets. The players also grab their bat bags which contain two baseball bats, cleats, glove, batting gloves, batting helmets, half empty sunflower seed bags, and empty water bottles.

The long march to the coach's truck to put away the Eagles baseball gear commences. The ritual is the same as it has been for more than 90 baseball games and practice sessions this season. Brent grabs his bat bag, catcher's equipment bag, and whiffle ball bucket. He walks past the throngs of people milling around the Lewis and Clark baseball facility. His legs don't seem to want to work and he wishes he was on a walking machine at the airport that helps people who are late for their airplane to get through the airport.

Angry, frustrated, tired, and emotionally exhausted from the pressure of losing the chance at a perfect regular season, and carrying all the Eagles equipment to his father's truck, Brent isn't crying anymore.

Hatred is bouncing around in Brent's head.

"I wish I could transform into Taz and just tornado spin the Warriors, umpires, fans, coaches, my parents, and myself for losing the game," Brent grumbles to himself.

He opens the back door to his family's blue Ford F-150 pickup truck and climbs into "his" seat. He closes his eyes and makes a wish that his parent's truck will be a safe zone from today's failure at the plate. A secret refuge of peace, a quiet spot where he can be showered in the never-ending love of his parents. He knows better. After a loss to Westside, there will be no silence and no protection from the "what-if" hate-filled demons.

The car ride home for Brent begins with a long blank distant stare out the backseat window with no emotion and no words. The raging anger from the strikeout has zapped all his energy like a remote control airplane falling out of the sky with dead batteries. Resting his head against the back window of the truck, and covered with the red clay diamond dust of the baseball diamond infield, Brent stews on the recently completed game versus Westside, and can't wait to face them again in the Championship game. He mumbles out loud, "Dude, what's up? You have got to be kidding me! I was BEAST this season. I watched every MLB Network training video, I hit 24 home runs this season, what is going on – HOW. DO. I. NOT. SWING. AT. THAT. PITCH!! Uggh!"

The chirping from the front seat of the Ford F-150 truck begins to slowly creep into the back seat like a marine layer coming in from the ocean onto a deserted island beach. The low-level disappointment parent clouds are rolling in. Time for Brent to take cover!

As predictable as tornado sirens—and just as loud—his parent's voiceboxes begin to hum and swirl with disapproval. "Seriously, Brent, what were you thinking out there?" says his mom. The first wave of dialogue from the front seat is a glancing blow off Brent's ears. It's a rhetorical question, and easy to play defense.

"Your mother is talking to you, Brent. AN-SWER HER!" yells his dad. The verbal storm clouds are building and it's approaching Category III levels of anger.

Brent's brain kicks into gear and begins to scream at his body, *"DUCK and COVER! Incom-*

ing verbal assault! Activate the defensive shield! Begin operation 'Clam Up'. Just take it, big boy, turn the other cheek. Above all else, do not make eye contact or it will be worse than a run-in with a hungry cobra!"

In the front seat, Brent's parents, Pablo and Kay, are now talking extremely loudly over the top of each other. "How much money has been wasted on new bats, new cleats, new gloves, new, new, new. What a waste! How much time have I wasted driving you back and forth to practice? All the Powerade we've bought, down the drain! All the sunflower seeds we have spit! I can't take it anymore!" comes the parental verbal barrage.

Brent's brain issues another urgent warning to the mouth, *"Say nothing, absolutely nothing, and begin praying the ride home goes faster than a speeding bullet!"*

His parents lob another noisy attack on the distraught 12-year-old's ears. His Mom and Dad's insistence on replaying the lowlights of the game slowly begins to light Brent's anger campfire. "You missed backing up first base. You took a pitch you were supposed to swing at," his mom continues, hardly taking a breath.

"I couldn't hear you pulling for your teammates when you were in the dugout," goes the lecture.

"Steady, big fella," says the brain to the body. *"I know you wish you had invented a tele-porter time machine to get us out of here... but, hang in there. Almost home,"* encourages the brain. Brent has been down the "replay game road" before, and it never ends well—it's always a dead end.

Brent's brain can sense the danger of the vocabulary fire getting out of control. It issues an all-points bulletin to the body: *"Deflect all incoming words. Shoulders, DO NOT SLOUCH! Eyes, DO NOT GLARE! Face, DO NOT WRIN-KLE! Eyebrows, DO NOT MOVE!"* Any lan-guage from the body that appears to be disre-spectful will increase the intensity of the parent verbal storm. *"Remain as calm as possible. Hang in there, everybody, we are almost home!"*

Anger and hatred are tormenting Brent. Everyone has a breaking point. Brent's disap-pointment breaks rank with his brain and he fights back, "If you could teach hitting, WE wouldn't be in this mess. Why didn't you yell at that umpire! We had terrible calls against us all day! What's the matter? Were you afraid of him?" Brent throws the challenge flippantly to the driver's seat of the family truck.

Now, Brent's dad, Pablo, goes completely batty. "Kylan doesn't throw more than 40 miles per hour. He's horrible! After you watched strike three, you started bawling like a little baby on the field! What is wrong with you! You embarrassed me and your mother!" he shouts from the front seat.

Now Kay throws a verbal assist to her husband as she screams at her son, "That's it, Brent Ryan, no video games! When we get home, you will take a shower and go straight to BED!"

Brent gathers himself, takes a deep breath, and calmly collects his return fire of nasty attitude. "Nothing to post on Pinterest, Facebook, Snapchat, and Instagram right now, MOM?" continues Brent in a disrespectful tone to his mother. The verbal battle royal comes to a close. The family truck moves over to the slow lane to exit the freeway and make its final descent into the neighborhood.

Brent slowly drifts back into baseball television dreamland, thinking about how he can't wait for the rematch with the Westside Warrior Little League team. The next game will be for the chance to play on ESPN, in front of the entire nation! For a brief moment, he ponders the thought of the ESPN initials standing for 'Every Sports Parent is Nuts'. True heartbreak is staring back at his parents in the rearview mirror. If they would just look, and feel what he feels.

No one wins the car ride battle. The youth baseball Player vs. Parent War will continue next baseball practice, next baseball game, and next baseball season.

Chapter 2

Yes, We Are Talking About Practice

Prior to their rematch for the Little League Championship versus the Westside Warriors on Saturday, the Eastside Eagles are about to conduct one last practice session.

"Mom, let's go! We are going to be late for practice! Come on!" Donnie yells from the garage as he frantically puts his overstuffed blue and black bat bag into his mom's Jeep Cherokee.

"Honey, relax, we have an hour 'til practice starts, and I'm helping your sister with her

spelling words," Donnie's mother, Megyn, replies calmly.

Donnie's voice is breaking up, and panic is
taking over, "Are you insane? If we don't leave
right now, I'll be the *last* Eagles player at practice—which means I'll start the Championship
game on the bench! We have to go right *now!*"

"Would you stop it!" his mother insists.
"Coach said practice starts at 6 p.m. and we will
be there at 6 p.m. Go get your baseball stuff together. After I'm done helping your sister, we
will go to your little practice."

Tears begin to well up under Donnie's sports
performance eye black. He comes face to face
with the realization that he will be "on time" for
practice. Every player on the Eastside Eagles
Little League team knows that if you are "on
time," then you are *late*. Donnie slowly turns to
his journal notebook, which all Eagles received
at the beginning of the season. Remembering
the first day Donnie met Coach Pablo at the
player-parent-coach preseason meeting feels
like just yesterday.

"Eagles players are expected to keep their
journal updated after each and every practice

during the season." Donny remembers Coach Pablo explaining this forcefully. "These journals are meant to keep important information. The team's secret steal and bunt signs are listed in this notebook. Mechanical batting swing reminders are written down to remind players during the season how to be prepared. Inspirational sayings are listed in the journal to help keep you motivated," Coach Pablo had instructed.

"In bold black ink, listed on **page 1** of the Eastside Eagles notebook, is the following:

Mental Toughness! Control the Controllables! No FEAR! Focus! Being a champion means giving everything you have got inside you and then just a little bit more effort!

"Keep this page of inspiring phrases handy, and commit them to memory this season," the coach of the Eastside Eagles Little League team had urged. Coach Pablo has been given the precious opportunity to lead a group of 12-year-old boys onto the baseball field to play a game.

Unable to hide from the fact he will be "on time" to practice, Donnie comes face to face with **page 2** of his team notebook. In Donnie's own

handwriting with dark black ink screaming up
at him like a neon sign bringing gamblers into
Las Vegas:

Don't be selfish. Don't be rude. If you arrive for meetings on time for your job when you get older then you are late. Be <u>early</u> to meetings and events with people, it is a sign you respect and value their time. Be <u>early</u> to practice. Be <u>early</u> to games. Respect yourself. Respect your teammates. Respect the game of baseball.

Donnie is dazed, like a prizefighter going for
the World Boxing Championship belt. *"How can
my mom not know how important this is to me!
I've told her how important it is to be early to
practice and games. I've told her a thousand
times about this on the car rides to and from
baseball since the second practice of the season!
We've got to be early. We've got to be early!
Why are we going to be 'on time' for the practice
before the Championship game!"* an angry Eagles player screams inside his head.

"Good grief! She is as lost as last year's
Easter egg," he mutters to himself in a trembling monotone whisper. He lets out a final

moan, "What is she thinking?" and heads toward the garage.

He does what his mom asks, and double
checks his bat bag prior to leaving for practice.
He looks into his bat bag (like all other Eagles
players do) to make sure he has: one neon orange Easton Mako 29-inch bat, one neon orange
Easton Maco-30 inch bat, one Rawlings Gamer
first base glove, one camo EvoShield wrist
guard, one EvoShield digital camo leg guard,
two Under Armour white batting gloves, batting
helmet with number 47 on the back, a package
of dill pickle David Sunflower seeds, a notebook
and pen, eye black stick, grape Powerade bottle,
and one black Wilson A2000 fielders glove for
when he's on the mound, pitching.

"Yup, I've got everything I need for practice,
*except a Bugatti Chiron Super Sports Car that
can go 260 miles per hour and gets me to the
field!*" he laughs.

Waiting for his mom to finish helping his
sister feels like waiting two hours at the ortho-
dontist to get a broken wire on braces fixed.
"This is getting ridiculous. My sister is stupid.
Why even waste the time on her, anyway? If my
mom doesn't hurry up, there is no way I'm going

to start the Championship game at first base!"
Donnie is pacing around the garage, talking out
loud to the storage boxes in the rafters.

Hatred and anger play demolition derby in
Donnie's head.

Donnie closes his eyes and can see the Eagles' lineup card hanging in the dugout before
the Championship game and there is NO DON-
NIE IN THE BATTING ORDER. NO DONNIE
STARTING AT FIRST BASE!

Meanwhile, Coach Pablo's truck barrels into
his parking space at the field at 4:33 p.m. Coach
is running a couple of minutes behind his
schedule because he needed to stop at the 7-11
convenient store for sunflower seeds. For more
than ten years during his baseball coaching
stint, the seeds must be original with lots of salt
and no fancy flavors. Coach is a baseball tradi-
tionalist with sunflower seeds. One large hand-
ful of seeds jammed into the right side of his
mouth, and then individual seeds expelled onto
the field. Repeating the process until the sunflower seed bag is empty.

A hidden "treasure" of being the coach's kid
on the baseball team is the duty of moving all

the Eagles team's gear between his family truck and the dugout before and after each practice and game.

"Brent, grab the ball bucket, catcher's gear bag, and my fungo bat out of the back of the truck," mumbles the coach, his dad, from a mouth overflowing with salty sunflower seeds.

"I've hauled enough gear to be a professional crab fisherman on the Bering Sea!" Brent thinks, as he wrestles the Eagles equipment to the practice field for the 97th time this season.

The parking lot at the practice field welcomes Eagles players, coaches, and parents. The kids slowly begin to work their way toward the diamond from the parking lot, like buffalo lumbering over the open prairie, looking for their next spot to graze.

"Hey, Bra, need some help with the gear?" offers Danny, Brent's teammate. Danny, the centerfielder, is a prototypical Eagles player. He's skinny and small, but with a big heart for the team. Danny loves his Eagles teammates and can't wait to get to the field. He is fearless in the outfield. Running into the fence to catch a fly ball in warm ups is not uncommon. He got the nickname "Triple D" because his teammates say that "Danny Digs Diving" in the outfield. Danny works hard at baseball and is one of the smartest kids in the classroom on the team. Danny is also the social butterfly of the team.

"No, Bro, I've got it, but thanks!" Brent calls back.

"Yo, Brent, my brother from another mother," says Todd, passing Brent in the parking lot on the way to the practice field. "Coach in a good mood, man? Or is he grumpy? Just want to know if I've got to do extra stretches to prepare to run all day or not, man?"

Todd plays third base for the Eastside Eagles. He's slow, and has been known to be razzed by teammates as "the Turtle." Todd does have sneaky baseball speed and knows the game backwards and forwards. He is not afraid of ground balls. He has taken several baseballs off his chin and in the cup. Todd is a quiet leader for the Eagles. He only gets fired up when the team is losing.

Twelve Eagles players usually know what to expect at practice, especially the practice before the Championship game. Since the beginning of the season, each Eastside baseball practice has covered pretty much the same basic topics— throw the baseball, catch the baseball, and hit the baseball, all with extreme focus on getting to the Championship game. The Eagles had hung on for a nail-biting 5 to 4 victory against the Capuchins, and the Eagles' next practice had been spent working on base running. Two hours of running the bases was enough to convince every Eagles player that running as fast as they can through first base on a ground ball would be a wise decision.

"Milkshake, what flavor did ya get today, Bro?" asks Jerald as they stroll through the outfield grass toward the dugout before practice begins.

"Berry. Man, you know me. I can't stand that other fake stuff. Gotta stay true, yo," replies Mitchell.

Mitchell, also known as "Milkshake," is the largest kid, pound for pound, on the team. At five feet eleven inches tall and just over 125 pounds, Mitchell arrives at every practice and game with a strawberry milkshake in hand. Mitchell is a loveable kid that always has a smile on his face off the baseball field. However,

41

for whatever unknown freakish reason, when he steps onto the baseball diamond, he can't help but cry. Mitchell cries a lot. Mitchell, however, is a great teammate. He is the one who has everyone over to his house to swim and to have sleep-over parties.

"Ha, you better pound that shake, kid! We be running tonight, and ya gonna hurl that berry shake all over this field, yo!" Jerald laughs, waving his finger at Mitchell's drink.

Jerald is the oldest player on the team, having a September 1st birthday. He is also the best pitcher. He has command of an incredible fastball, and changes up pitches to hitters with a side arm knuckleball that freezes batters in their stance. The pitch is simply described as "wicked hard" throughout the League. Jerald is a leader in the dugout, always firing up his teammates. Jerald loves baseball, and dreams of playing in the major leagues. He is always cracking jokes and is the life of any party.

The clock on Coach Pablo's iPhone displays 5:40 p.m. Mountain Time. "All right, that's enough fooling around! It's time to get to work. Gloves on the bench, not on the ground, and if I see a glove in the dirt, you'll run for the entire practice! Treat your gloves well, and they will treat you well!" he yells.

"You got it, Coach" says Dallas, as he flies past Pablo at Mach 5 supersonic speed, nearly knocking him over.

Dallas is tall and skinny for a twelve-year-old, and he roams the outfield like a gazelle. Dallas has five older brothers and is always competing for attention. Dallas longs to play in the infield; however, no matter how hard he tries, he just can't get the hang of fielding ground balls. He is a natural left fielder. He is a great switch hitter, but he lacks the confidence to try it in a game. One of the fastest ball players on the team, Dallas also plays hockey, basketball, football, and runs track.

Coach Pablo begins his practice with the team stretching out in the shallow portion of left field between the infield and outfield. A series of 25 stretches for the arms and legs is done in military unison with clear cadence for team unity. No player misses a stretch routine, and all players give 100 percent attention to the detailed sequence of motions.

"One, two, three, One, two, three, One, two, three, and switch!" goes the rhythmic humming of the ball players.

"All day, baby, I got this. See this form, my fine feathered friends?" KC calls out to all his Eagles teammates during warmups.

KC is the team's shortstop. His name could easily be Captain America instead of KC. He is the best-dressed player on the team. KC shows up to baseball games in a perfectly ironed baseball uniform. His uniform is always as white and clean as fresh-driven snow. KC uses gel to keep every hair on his head in place. KC asked for three brand-new hats during the season because he doesn't like to have dirty gear. The ball must be attracted to KC's good looks in the batter's box—KC leads the team in getting hit by the pitch.

After stretching, each of the coaches performs a well-rehearsed motivational sermon. Coach Pablo's practice speech tonight will hit the themes of focusing on every play, work hard, give maximum effort, keep your attitude edge, and the classic "Have fun" final order.

Brent is a veteran at listening to coaches' speeches. He's heard at least 500 renditions of the same talk, and can give the conclusion to them before the coach finishes. Brent easily senses when the pre-Championship Game final practice speech reaches its intended crescendo. "Get ready, fellas, it's just about time to get practice started," Brent whispers to his team-mates as that moment approaches.

"Stay focused. Flush bad plays! Give maxi-mum effort on every pitch. Everyone ready? Let's get an 'Eagles' on three—one, two, three, EAGLES!" says Coach Pablo. It's their signal to leap to their feet and give high fives to each oth-er, grab their water bottles, and head to the next phase of practice.

The players reach for their gloves from their bat bags, partner up, and begin to loosen up their arms. Short distances between throws to start with, and then gaining distance as they warm up their arms. If or when a ball hits the ground during warm ups, a penalty is paid. The entire team is responsible for the fine.

"Manny, you wanna warm up?" asks Joey.

Joey starts most games in right field. However, he finishes the game on the bench. Joey is the classic uninterested youth baseball player that can be found watching squirrels run up trees, swatting at bugs, and picking dandelions during ball games to keep himself entertained. Joey doesn't have a passion for baseball. He knows his mom makes him participate to gain friends and get exercise. Joey is a tremendous athlete. He dominates on the basketball court and football field. He has pure raw talent and will go far in other sports besides baseball, as long as he focuses on his school work.

Manny quickly answers Joey, "Si, Si!" Manny is a short stocky second baseman. Born to play the position, he is light years ahead of kids his age when playing defense. He loves to turn double plays, and instinctively knows where to go on each play, as if he can see into the future. He is blessed with loads of talent. Manny, however, does carry emotional baggage that yields to crying in almost every game. He places a tremendous amount of pressure on his small shoulders. He has a unique will to win. Manny leads the team in ripped uniforms, three, as he plays the game hard and is always on the ground.

Throwing and catching the baseball is not going well for the Eagles at the beginning of tonight's practice.

"Brent, how many balls hit the ground during warm ups?" barks Coach Pablo, his dad.

Brent and the entire team respond in perfect unison, "Four!"

"You know what to do—let's get after it, so we can start to clean up your mess from our last ballgame during this practice. Hurry up! You move as slow as little old ladies at the beauty salon! We're burning daylight," grumbles the coach. The 12 young ball players begin to form a line along the third base foul line, all in white uniform pants, EASTSIDE hats, black molded Under Armour cleats, and matching practice jerseys that say *"IT'S AN ATTITUDE!"*

"Put your gloves down on the ground. Get in your batting stance, and GO!" screams the coach as he watches his team sprint in a line towards second base. "What!!! Are you kidding me, no sliding? Are you worried your mommy isn't going to wash those pretty white pants! Back in line and do it again! Hurry up, Brent, you lazy sissy!" hollers his dad.

"Need a barf bag yet, Bro?" whispers Jerald to Milkshake as they head back for another wind sprint.

After the fourth time sprinting to pay their penalty for throwing and catching mistakes, and another three sprints for not sliding, Coach Pablo yells, "Alright! I can't take any more of this! It's too hard to watch! Go to your positions in the field."

Mitchell puts his arm around Jerald as he bends down to get his glove and gasps, "Wow! If we did one more sprint, Bra, this field was going to get to taste *ALL* my berry shake."

Each player on the Eastside Eagles Little League squad knows his primary defensive position. They were assigned spots after the third practice of the season. The players sprint out to their positions on the ball diamond— all of them remembering, like snow geese heading south for the winter, where to go.

"Donnie, Hector, and Reese! Get helmets on!" Coach Pablo barks. Donnie, Hector, and Reese start most games on the bench, and then are substituted in to meet minimum play requirements according to League rules.

"I knew it! Stupid mom and stupid sister," steams Donnie under his flat-billed hat, pulled down over his eyebrows.

"Sorry, fellas. Stay focused. We will need you guys in the Championship game," says Brent to his three teammates as they pass each other in opposite directions. Brent heads to the field, and Donnie, Hector, and Reese head to the dugout. Brent has his catcher's glove, and extra baseballs for the coach to hit infield and outfield practice. Brent is one of the skinniest players on the team. A majority of Eagles players weigh less than 75 pounds and stand less than five feet tall. Brent loves playing catcher because he receives the ball on every play. Brent is the most competitive kid on the team, hating to lose a game even more than he likes winning a game.

Coach Pablo pulls out his aluminum fungo bat from the catcher's gear bag and begins to hit fly balls to the outfield. The infield/outfield defensive session should last thirty minutes—or longer, if the team can't focus.

Tonight and almost every night of practice during the season, the team will spend more than an hour on defensive drills. The Eagles are a great defensive fielding team in comparison to other ball clubs. However, Coach Pablo does not like errors and wants a perfect fielding session.

"Perfect" in baseball is a very rare commodity. Only 23 Major League Baseball *perfect* games have been pitched out of 209,000 games played in the entire history of the professional game. Hall of Fame major league managers know that baseball is a game of failure. Professional baseball executives know the game is about overcoming failure. More flaws than perfection is the norm for the game of baseball. How to minimize mistakes, maximize positive plays, build "team first" attitude, and immediately focus on the next baseball play after a mistake are the golden keys to successful ball clubs.

"Everyone, hit the dugout," Coach Pablo stammers in frustration. Donnie, Hector, and Reese now have company. "If we want any chance to win the Championship game this weekend, we will need to be focused on the field! We've got to play better defense," the Coach lectures.

"Heck of a catch in warm ups, Triple D!" Sitting next to each other on the dugout bench, KC whispers to Danny, "Robbing that home run Coach thought he'd hit was BEAST, yo!"

"Jerald, Reese, and Donnie, sprint to the bullpen to practice pitching! Work on changing speeds and hitting spots. Get your location under control," orders Coach Pablo. "It's going to be important against Gannon, Butler, and Kylan from Westside," he reminds them. "Everyone else, grab your bats!" Coach starts Phase Three of the night's practice.

Hitting practice takes many forms. Players hit whiffle balls off a tee, oversized balls are soft tossed from the side, live hitting on the field, and one-on-one session with the teams hitting Coach behind the backstop. Batters work on hitting fastballs, curveballs, and off-speed change-up pitches at each station. Batting practice is normally an hour long; however, with the Championship game on the horizon, tonight the team will hit for ninety minutes.

"Man, I love pounding the rock! My neon orange Mako bat has been on fire all year long!" Todd calls out as he kills the ball during his batting practice session.

The hitting drills go well, and the team is focused. No surprise, the hitting phase of practice goes well—it's the best part of baseball for kids. There is no other feeling like it on the planet—having the walk off game winning hit!

"Stay relaxed at the plate," Coach Pablo reminds Joey. "Remember, kid, you're trying to hit a round ball with a round bat while it's moving at 60 miles per hour. It's a hard sport, and hitting is a hard thing to do."

Shagging fly balls in the outfield during hitting practice, Dallas sees Joey and says to his teammates, "Man, Joey is up at the plate grunting like one of those Russian weightlifters trying to bench press 500 pounds. He's got to take it easy or he's going to pop a stitch!"

"Worthless bat, I'm horrible," mumbles Joey as he chokes back tears.

In the quest for baseball hitting's Holy Grail, parents shell out top dollar for a thirty minute session with a private hitting guru, usually a former minor league player to obtain extra magical hits for their kid. Coach Pablo is thinking to himself, *"How's that 50 bucks for private hitting sessions, twice a week for six*

months, going for Joey's parents now? Instead of worrying about getting a baseball college scholarship, they should take that money and contribute to his 529 Education Savings Account."
After each Eagles player rotates through live hitting on the field, it's time for the final phase of practice—running the bases.

"Let's go, Brent! It's time for you and the other Eagles superstars to run the bases!" A deep laughing boom comes from his dad.

The Eagles assistant coaches chime in. "We've got to run the bases well to have any chance in the Championship game. As soon as you see the ball hit the dirt and get past the catcher it's RUN time! Let's go! Let's go!"

"Oh, snap, I thought we were done running," quivers Milkshake.

With a wry smile, Jerald dares his teammate, "Hey, Donnie, you run behind Milkshake during this drill!"

The players spend the next 25 minutes running around the bases. Every Eagles player practices stealing second and third base. The

Eagles conclude practice by running all the way around the bases, just in case an inside the ballpark home run is to be had in the Championship game.

By now, parents have been milling around the practice field since 5:00 p.m. and are getting restless to go home. Behind the dugout, several moms form gossip huddles to talk about how they can't stand the white uniform pants. "We need gray pants like Westside. Their stains come out much easier, according to Kylan's mom."

"This coach is definitely trying to re-live his glory days. Have you seen him in his coach's uniform? Omigosh—what a fashion disaster!"

"I swear, sometimes I think he is out on that field just so he can put on a glove and try to play baseball with the boys like some ten-year-old kid. It really is embarrassing for him." "The way he talks to these boys is just not nice. I can't wait for this season to be over," say the moms, sounding altogether similar to a gaggle of squawking geese.

Meanwhile, the dads are having a field day, second-guessing the coaches' decisions to steal in the first inning of the last game. "Has he seen Jerald run? This guy is lucky to have his team playing for the Championship game. He always bats his kid first—what kind of a joke is that? I can't wait for the League season to be over, so we can get started with the summer travel baseball team. That team has it together!" sing the jealous dads in perfect harmony.

Practice concludes, nearing the 9:00 p.m. hour. Eleven of the 12 Eagles players have been at the fields since 5:05 p.m. Players pile into their family cars for the ride home, quick shower, late dinner, and homework. Then, off to bed to dream about baseball and the Championship on the horizon.

Chapter 3

Stats, Stats—Everywhere Stats

The aluminum bleachers directly behind home plate on Field 5 at the Lewis and Clark Little League Baseball Complex buzz with pre-game chitter chatter, similar to tailgates at Southeastern Conference college football games. SEC football tailgate food is delicious. But the Lewis and Clark bleachers prior to the Championship game have a foul stench, and offer only heartburn to all who eat from their gossip feast.

"Did you know *my* Manny's On Base Percentage (OBP) is .478? That's the third highest percentage on the team, yet he only gets 25% of

the plate appearances! That crazy Coach Pablo
still has him hitting last in the batting order!"
says Manny's mom, talking out loud to absolutely
no one, while hiding behind her iPad.

Not to be outdone, Joey's dad chimes in, "Not
only is *my* Joey the fastest player on the team, he
is also the best pitcher on this team, *but* he never
gets to start a game. He never gets to pitch in a
game, for crying out loud! He has a *great* fastball.
We bought a brand new radar gun and clocked my
son throwing 35 miles per hour! He could strike
out three kids in a row, *if* he wanted to. If you
could see his curveball, you would say he's headed
straight for a major league contract. What a pitch!
This daddy-coach doesn't know what he's doing.
If they want to win this Championship game, he's
got to give the ball to *my* Joey to start the game
today," Joey's prideful dad rambles on, offering
his pre-game keys to the spectator stats gossip
stew.

"No, no, no. Reese leads the team in striking
out batters with runners in scoring position with
55 K's. No one in this county can hit his pitches.
After I've been talking with him and giving him
pointers, his WHIP is now below 2!" retorts
Reese's uncle. He is anxiously analyzing the

Eastside Eagles pre-game warm up drills on Field 5 to see who will be the starting pitcher.

"Where's the starting lineup for today's game? I can't tell from what's going on out there if my son is going to start at the pitcher position. Where does this loser coach have my son batting in the lineup? His slugging percentage is .550 over the last ten games. He better have him leading off today. He takes the first pitch every time, and is the most patient hitter on the team," scolds another dad, leaning against the side of the cold bleachers.

The head coach is tardy bringing over the lineup card to the scorekeepers in the bleachers, which only adds to the crowd's tense behavior. Despite the team's 15-1 record, the comments and advice for Coach Pablo keep rolling in like a dusty haboob in the Arizona desert.

"Would you look at this! Mitchell has his first baseman's glove on during the pre-game infield drills. Good grief, is he going to start *Mitchell* at first base? What a joke. The kid can't throw the ball from first to third. It's going to be a long six innings today, especially when he starts crying in the first inning," Hector's grandpa predicts.

"Can you see who's in the bullpen warming up?" Jerald's younger brother asks, asking his question to anyone who might answer.

Brent's oldest brother responds, "Yeah, Brent and Jerald are playing catch in the bullpen. Looks like Jerald might be getting the start today."

Groans and complaints reverberate throughout the stands, like a seismograph going off announcing a magnitude 7.0 earthquake. The crowd is eager to see the starting lineup card for today's game. Moms, dads, aunts, uncles, grandparents, and siblings take turns pestering the two Eagles scorekeepers where their son—their favorite superstar player—is in the batting lineup, and which position in the field he is going to be playing.

The two scorekeepers for today's Championship game between the Eastside Eagles and the Westside Warriors play an important part in keeping the official record of the contest. The official record also includes the players statistics recorded during the game. Parents follow their son's baseball stats like a lost person leaving a trail of popcorn trying to get out of the forest. All the Eagle's parents anxiously follow their son's baseball stats, to argue who's the best kid on the team in which statistical category.

Brent's mom is the official scorekeeper for the Championship game. She has the responsibility of interacting with the home plate umpire, in case there is a question regarding how many balls and strikes or how many outs there are in an inning (just in case the umpire forgets).

Dallas's mom keeps track of the action during the game through the electronic scorebook. The electronic version, which can be viewed online by fans, parents, and anyone with internet access, is fertile ground for mischief. The electronic version of the players stats are never 100% accurate. Eastside Eagles parents analyze, with bated breath, their child's stats on the electronic score-book during every game of the season. There is no shortage of opinions on who should start and where in the batting order or at what position in the field a kid should be, based upon the electron-ic stats.

"Yo, Manny, how come you haven't joined our private group on the game Clan of Trolls, yet?" Reese asks, as they play catch prior to the Cham-pionship game.

"When my OBP went below 500, it was off to the private hitting instructor I go. I don't have time for anything but homework, practice, private hitting practice, and sleep. Oh, and maybe every once in a while, some food!" says Manny.

"That sucks, Bra," says Reese.

"It's not really *THAT* bad... and I can live with all that garbage, *but* what really makes me angry is my mom took away my iPod!" screams Manny.

Reese shrugs his shoulders and says, "That is crazy stupid silly."

Dallas and KC are playing catch right next to Manny and Reese. Dallas adds to the Eagles players' pre-game conversation while tossing the baseball back and forth. "That's nothing, kid, you got it easy. You know what's tough?" challenges Dallas.

"What's that, Triple D?"

Dallas jumps up to grab a wild throw from KC. "Turtle over there," he answers, pointing his index finger in the direction of his teammate, "keeps getting on base in front of me, which is great. *HOWEVER*, when I hit a bomb off the pitcher and it goes to the fence, little Turtle is ssssoooo slow he costs me my RBI stats. I'm getting yelled at during dinner because I don't drive in enough runs on this team!"

"Sorry, Bro," mumbles Turtle. He is bummed out and it shows in his voice and on his face.

Statistics run the family priority to-do list during the baseball on and off seasons. Player statistics are evaluated, contemplated, pondered, and fretted over, but very rarely rejoiced over. Eastside and Westside parents do not like each other; however, they all agree on one thing—their boy's baseball statistics can "always" be improved!

Brent remembers, all too well, his mom's postgame recap during dinner of the very first game of the season. "With more hustle, you would have gotten a hit in the fourth inning instead of a ground out. Your batting average with runners in scoring position would be higher!" his mom's commentary replays in his head.

Coach Pablo walks past Brent as he leaves pre-game warmups with the team to go talk to Kay, his wife and veteran baseball mom.

"Hey, Dad!" Brent calls to his Dad as he walks past the team toward the bleachers. "I think you should start Jerald today on the mound. He looks great in warmups. His wicked knuckleball is..." Brent is cut off by his father.

"Stay focused on your fielding and throwing. Worry about your hitting. Leave the lineup card and all game decisions to me. I know what I'm doing. I've been at this a lot longer than you have!" yells his Dad, making a beeline toward his wife.

"What a jerk. I hate that he's the manager of this stupid team," mumbles Brent to himself as he walks toward the dugout.

"He's not a jerk, Brent," says Jerald.

Startled that Jerald overheard him, Brent reacts. "What?"

"He's not a jerk, Bro. He's your coach. He's your dad. Gotta forgive and forget, kid!" says Jerald.

"Easy for you to say. I've got to live with him!"

"You want to know what a jerk really is?" Before Brent can answer, Jerald says, "A jerk is that clown Butler over there, on the Warriors team. I go to school with him, and he is a 'Class -A' JERK. We're talking J.E.R.K."

"Go on and get all your feelings about him being a jerk out in the open. Make sure not to leave out the part about forgive and forget!" Brent reminds him with a grin.

"Shut up, Bro. Anyway, Butler goes all over school telling everyone that the Eagles SUCK and the Warriors are going to beat us like a rented mule," says Jerald.

"A rented mule?" echoes Brent, with a puzzled expression on his face.

"Like I said, he's a jerk. I have no idea what the heck he means by it, and I don't think he does, either. Anyway, no one listens to him, he has no friends. He keeps popping off about how his fielding percent is 1,000. He's never dropped a ball. He's never made an error," says an irritated Jerald.

"Seriously. That kid has problems," says Brent.

"The Warriors have *millions* of problems," concludes Jerald.

Having completed their pre-game warmup tosses, Dallas, KC, Manny, and Reese continue their statistics conversation in the dugout.

"Look, Bro, you have no idea what "rough" is when your dad starts down the stats dead-end road. My dad can remember *every* pitch and *every* situation during *every* game," says Reese, his voice rising. His anger is growing as he recalls each detail. "I was on the mound pitching in *the* game and *I* don't remember every pitch!" Reese's voice is getting louder.

"I hear you, Reese Man the Beast Man," says Manny.

"My uncle yelled at me because five games ago my WHIP (Walks + Hits per Inning Pitched) went over 2," Reese remembers. "He would not get off my back. Every single time I saw him, he would bring up that my WHIP was above 2. Give me a break. I'm pitching my tail off! It's not my fault the lousy umpire called 'ball four' on a pitch right down the middle of the plate!" Reese finally yells.

In unison, Dallas and KC exclaim, "Parents are stats-crazy, yo!"

All four players yell, "Jinx!"

"Hi, Honey," Coach Pablo greets his wife after leaving his team's warmups. She has a lawn chair unfolded next to home plate, just off to the side of the toxic attitude bleachers. Her phone is at the ready, to reply to texts from friends and family that "need" updates on the Championship game action.

"You ready for today? How do the boys look? You got a lineup card for me, yet?" Kay rattles off her questions.

"I'm guessing our bleachers are in their usual form today. Does everyone have suggestions for me on who to play at which position and who to bat in which order?" replies Coach Pablo crossly.

"Same story as all the other games," says Kay. "You've got lots of baseball moms and dads giving lineup card help based on the electronic scorebook stats they see online. You know they take those stats as gospel. They've got no idea those stats are not 100% accurate and can be skewed."

"Just once, I'd like to have a parent say they would sacrifice their son's individual statistics for the good of their team," Coach Pablo murmurs to his wife.

Kay looks at her husband with a slight smile. "You'll hit the Powerball Jackpot, first, Honey," she sighs.

Parents love individual statistics they can fantasize about. Player stats are a false idol, worshiped by far too many sports parents and fans. But, coaches love 12 kids all pulling together for the team to win a Championship.

Chapter 4

The Line Up Card

Championship Saturday finally arrives for Brent. It's the perfect chance for him to redeem himself for losing the regular season game, and a chance at a perfect season against Westside. He's been dreaming of playing in the Championship game all season. With a win in the Championship game he will be able to play his next game on ESPN.

"Game Day, BABY!" Brent says to himself, with a clenched fist raised high in the air as he bolts downstairs for breakfast.

As Brent glides down the staircase, he sees his older brother on the couch with the clicker firmly in hand. He's watching highlights from last night's Red Sox vs. Yankees game on the Major League Baseball network.

"Hey, Brent, dude, watch this replay... it's totally sick," says his older brother. "The Yankees batter is so angry at getting hit by the Red Sox pitcher that he chucks his bat at him. It is crazy!"

"I've been that angry before," Brent thinks, remembering, all too well, his fury three weeks ago. It was a game the Eagles won 21 to 5, versus the Mud Cats. Brent had struck out with the bases loaded. His dad, Coach Pablo, yelled so loud at him that crows, watching the action from their perch on an electric power pole, flew away at lightning speed. Brent had wished he could fly away with them.

Anger throws a curveball at Brent, interrupting the joyous beginning to his Championship Saturday. "Should've thrown my bat at Dad," fumes Brent under his breath.

His mom's cheerful voice interrupts his thoughts. "Good morning, dear, are you ready for today? Who've you got starting the game at pitcher?" Brent's mom, Coach Pablo's wife, is the number one fan of the Eastside Eagles and longtime scorekeeper for the team. She sips on her double half-caffeine half-nonfat mocha while cooking breakfast.

Brent waits for his dad to answer. Nothing happens. Finally, Brent says, "Hey." He wonders if his mom even remembers the conversation he had with her last night when he told her how nervous he is about today's huge Championship game. He wishes she would offer him a hot cup of cocoa with whipped cream and some reassuring words. But she hardly seems to notice he came into the room. She is still trying to get his dad to talk to her.

Brent's dad is in a zombie-like walk to the coffeemaker located on the kitchen counter.

"Hello, hello, anyone home? It's a simple question. Who's starting?" his mom prods, trying again to fill the silence.

Coach Pablo has the Eagles magnetic lineup card, iPad, and team scorebook in front of him as he prepares for the Lewis and Clark Little League Championship game against their rival,

the Westside Warriors. The Warriors are the
only team they've lost to this season. He thinks
to himself, "That team is not better than mine
... they only have three players that can hurt
my team."

Brent sees that his dad is not hearing him
or his mom, even as the kids and the television
set play in the background. His dad doesn't hear
any noises except those bouncing back and forth
inside his head, screaming to play this player,
how the pitching matchups should go, and what
order to put the players in the batting lineup.

"Hey! It's been like this for 16 games this
season! Answer me when I'm talking to you!"
screams an annoyed yet predictable baseball
mom. Brent figures her feeling is similar to
walking up to the Redbox machine looking for
the latest movie release on Friday night and
knowing it's not going to be there, but you try
anyway.

Startled, his dad responds, "Oh, huh, sorry,
just wondering about different starting lineup
combinations for today's game."

"You've been going back and forth all week
on that lineup, and you change your mind after

each practice. Have you settled on anything yet?" Brent's mom Kay tries to be patient and keep the conversation going. Brent hopes to engage his dad in a positive conversation, but he knows the tension will rise and might even end up in an argument.

"KC and Todd both hit the ball great in practice this week, but Hector's grandfather is in town this weekend and Jerald has been throwing great the last couple of games, while Brent is our best hitter on the team... ugh," mutters a frustrated Coach Pablo. "I know the boys are prepared and they have been working hard all spring. They are ready, I can feel it. I have prepared them as well as I can. My pitchers are fine on their pitch count requirement for the days of rest between games rules. Our hitting is on fire. The team is ready. I think Westside will start Butler at pitcher and try to close the game with Kylan. I know if the boys can get on base, we will be able to steal on Gannon when he's behind the plate," says a befuddled Coach. He suddenly realizes he is talking to no one, as his wife has left the room to refill her "foofoo" coffee drink.

"Um, Dad? Are you talking to me? Mom is in the other room." Brent asks cautiously.

Brent worries. Isn't the Coach supposed to have this all figured out by game day? "Well, Dad, what you always say, ..." Brent begins, meaning to encourage his nervous father.

But his mother interrupts, chiming in from the next room. "You'll be fine. You are the best coach in that league! Just don't let the parents get to you, and like you tell the kids—Flush it!" yells Brent's mom from the kitchen.

After his dad has another round of coffee and half a bite of burnt toast smothered in peanut butter, Brent sees that his father is back to staring at the piles of scorebooks, practice notes and stats filling the computer screen. Like sinners on their knees, praying to God for forgiveness, Coach knows the winning lineup card for the game is locked in the paper stack, if it would just talk back to him! Brent gives up on the hope that they can start the day with cheerful conversation or exchange words of encouragement. They all could use some of that, he is quite sure.

"Start Don Juan," Coach says, mumbling Donnie's nickname, "or start Milkshake Mitchell at first base? Both are decent defensively. One cries more than the other in tight ballgames, need someone who can make two plays and can think on his feet," again talking to no one in particular, his father's voice careens off the living room table.

His father's cell phone rings. The dial tone is the U.S. Army's Calvary's charge theme music coming from a bugle, blaring through the tiny cell phone speakers. Brent cringes. He knows these last minute phone calls can throw his father into a whirlwind of irritation.

"Hello, Coach, it is Donnie's mom, Megyn," comes out of the phone receiver.

"Hi, Megyn, what can I do for you?"

"Well, my daughter needs to be at dance practice and then piano lessons and I know you want the boys at the game an hour before it starts but that just isn't going to work for me. Do you think the game is going to start on time? Any chance you can get this game moved back, say 30 minutes?" inquires Donnie's mom.

"I'm not..." Coach Pablo doesn't get to finish his sentence.

"It's just this one time. I don't have time to get him a hot dog, chips, and cookie before the game, and you don't allow food in the dugout during the game, and those games always run late anyway, and I don't see what the big deal is," interrupts a squawking and irate mother.

"The League isn't going to move the Championship game back. Would you like me to pick up Donnie on my way to the field?" asks the Coach. He knows exactly where Donnie lives. He's been to the house a dozen times this season to pick up or drop off Donnie for practices and games.

"Well, I might take you up on it, but we do go to *all* of Donnie's games and practices, so I'm making him go to his sister's dance and piano today. He needs to support his sister because it's not always about baseball!" the Little League mother blurts out. She sounds ticked off.

"I'll make sure Donnie is on the lineup card, but if you can't make it in time for the game, please make sure to call me," says Coach.

"Fine!" replies Megyn, triumphantly.

Brent's dad hits the red End button on his phone. Now he knows her phone number will not show up again on his phone prior to the game.

If, by some fluke, the coach's cell phone were to bugle again, it will be deep in the Coach's sling bag with the lineup cards, pencils, rulebook, volunteer umpire certification card, medical release, and volunteer application forms for all Eagles players and parents, the Snack Shack volunteer schedule, lock combinations to the equipment storage sheds at the Lewis and Clark Little League Field, brush, and clicker in case the umpires forget theirs, and most importantly, a jumbo bag of original salted David Sunflower seeds.

"Who was on the phone, Dad?" asks Brent, rushing over to the table to eat his breakfast. He's dressed in full Eagles uniform, including his hat.

"Don Juan's—Donnie's—mother, asking if the game could be changed today," replies his dad through tight lips.

"No way!" Brent's head snaps up to look at his dad, his nerves on edge. *"We are* playing the

game today, right?" he anxiously demands. He
can't believe what he just heard.

"Absolutely! The weather forecast is for sun
and no clouds," his dad reassures him. "Try and
eat some more eggs and bacon." Brent's father
tries to regain his focus on the Eagles starting
lineup, and who will pitch in which order during
the Championship game.

*"Donnie will be late to the game and in a
panic. It will take him a few innings to settle
down,"* Pablo thinks to himself. *"I wonder which
parents let their child stay up to watch the Tonight Show last night."*

Brent's dad must be careful to survey all the
Eagles players during warm ups to see which
players are alert and ready for the game. A good
week of practice can't overcome a chocolate do-
nut breakfast and sleep deprivation.

Championship Saturday throughout the
state of Idaho is a special celebration. Young
ball players in each age division across league
borders will get a chance to play for a Championship ring. Today is THE DAY players ages 9
to 14 get the chance to be called CHAMPIONS!

Twenty-four 12-year-old boys from the Little League Westside and Eastside teams roll out of bed on Championship game day Saturday to the warm buzz of a pressure cooker starting up. Nervous parents of all age ranges feed the pressure cooker throughout the morning their special recipe of verbal goulash. The boys' excitement of playing in the Championship game is displayed in their first act of the day—jumping out of bed and sprinting to the closet to put on their baseball uniforms.

"Mom, where is my belt for my uniform pants?" screams a Westside Warrior player. Anger takes a turn at increasing the pressure cooker heat under the nervous stew.

"If you can't even get dressed by yourself, how on earth are you going to be in the starting lineup for the game today?" snaps the player's mom. "Take off your jersey top while you eat breakfast! You're going to get it messy. You are not focused today," she continues in annoyance. The pressure cooker keeps chugging along through breakfast, builds a little more steam during the car ride to the field, and finishes with a final salvo as the Little League player is dropped off at the Lewis and Clark Baseball Complex for pre-game warmups.

"You know, if you win today, you get to play on ESPN, so don't screw it up," is the unnecessary reminder an adoring son hears from his clueless baseball father.

Brent's dad ponders his final thoughts on who will start for the Championship game versus Westside. Brent's father comes from a family legacy of baseball coaches. Coach Pablo's dad, Brent's grandfather, was a Navy Seal and a no-nonsense father, as well as a volunteer baseball coach. When Coach Pablo played ball for his dad many years ago, he had been constantly reminded about every mistake he made. *"Quit crying right now or I'll give you something to really cry about!"* Brent's father recalls his dad saying. Brent's granddaddy never saw Brent play baseball. He died prior to Brent's first tee ball season, but he had spoken harsh words to his son, Pablo, when he was starting to learn to play. *"If you can't hit a baseball, you have no business being out here."* A haunting memory now hatefully whispers in Coach Pablo's ear. Somehow, he can still hear those angry words, *"I'm furious with you—get off my baseball field right now!"*

Brent's father wishes he had forgiven his dad for the mean words and the way he was treated by his dad, both on and off the baseball field, before he passed away. Brent's dad turned into a classic, yelling, screaming manager, just like *his* dad. He's hard-core, with a very angry, old-school managing style of baseball. The style of coaching he grew up under is the same style he now uses with the Eastside Little League Eagles. He makes no bones about his desire to win Little League baseball games and uses loud angry-sounding instructions to get his will accomplished. He demands perfection and attention to detail from his ballplayers and assistant coaches. His team is prepared, and he expects 100% energy, effort, and attitude at all times, both on and off the baseball field.

Brent's dad continually battles angry demons from his own baseball playing days long since gone by. They still have a way of haunting him even now as a team manager against local Little League and travel ball rivals. He's driven to win, a trait his own father, Brent's grandfather, pounded home his entire baseball playing career. He gets angry with his ballplayers' lack of focus. Because he gives his very best, he demands *his* players give their very best. Brent's dad does *not* forgive and forget.

Coach Pablo begins his final descent into the lineup card landing zone, and it sounds similar in his head to the flight attendant's announcement prior to landing a plane, "Ladies and gentleman, we've begun our final descent into Boise, Idaho. Please fasten your seat belts, put your tray table in the upright and locked position, and power down all electronic devises. We will be on the ground soon. Welcome to Boise."

The head coach sets his team lineup card by using a combination of gut feeling, awareness of the game day mental makeup of the players, strategy of the game, kid's ability, relatives from out of town, attendance, and past experience.

The coach is keenly aware that all parents, grandparents, opposing teams, fans, and his player's eyes are on him to see how he sets his lineup card. The same eyeballs will be on the coach during each pitch of the game and each strategic move he makes. All of the coaches' decisions are consistently judged through a second-guessing prism the size of the Great Pyramid of Giza in Egypt.

Brent's dad pulls out the lineup card from his manager's gear bag, reaches for his lucky blue Bic pen, and begins the starting lineup:

Batting First, wearing number 1, the catcher—Brent.

The number 1 and three-year running un-
disputed objection to Coach Pablo's Eastside
Eagles starting lineup is the fact he starts his
son at catcher and bats him first in the order for
every game.

"His kid always hits *first* in the batting order," come the catcalls from the Eagles fans.

Brent has heard the same criticism from the
Eagle's parents all season. He has the highest
batting average and is the best hitter on the
team; but because he is the coach's son, the fans
see it as unfairness.

"I hate being thought of as a teacher's pet!"
Brent's anger is the fuel that drives him to be
the best hitter in the entire state of Idaho.

To the objective baseball viewer, and espe-
cially the opposing team's managers, Coach
Pablo's son is the best player on the Eastside
Eagles. Brent loves baseball, dreams baseball,

and wants nothing more than to play baseball all day and night long. Parents who find fault with Brent hitting first in the lineup forget the fact that Brent's dad manages the team *because* his son *is* the best player on the team.

Coming in a strong second in parental objections to Coach Pablo's starting lineup for the Championship game (actually all Eagles games) is every parent's belief that their son should play shortstop. Irrelevant is the fact there can only be one shortstop on the field at a time— but, eleven sets of parents vote their child the starter for the game.

Batting Fourth and playing shortstop, number 19, is KC.

"If my son doesn't get to start at shortstop, he'll never be on the all-star team. He just *has* to play shortstop," come several groans from stands.

Batting Eighth and starting in Right Field, number 23 – Joey.

Akin to getting leprosy, start a youngster in right field, and all bloody war will break out in the stands.

"Right field! Right field! My son doesn't play right field. What is this half-baked coach thinking?" will be nasty calls coming from Joey's family.

A young ball player can feel the anger from his parents for getting assigned to play right field. The disappointment from his mom and dad for playing right field is a tremendous burden. The player slowly marches past first and second base on his way to the electric chair—the dreaded right field position.

The Coach is aware of these wrong ideas. *"Every year, the same thing which totally amazes me, is how and where this ideology got born, and that right field is for the worst baseball player, is pathetic. The right fielder must have the strongest arm in the outfield, ability to catch a fly ball, no easy task in youth baseball, be fast to backup plays at first base in case of overthrowing errors and be fearless to run into the fence—both fair and foul territory—to catch a ball,"* thinks Coach Pablo.

Coach Pablo is also keenly aware of the Eagles players' relatives that have traveled great distances to watch the Championship game.

"Coach, oh, Coach Pablo. I'm KC's mom. Do you remember me telling you my third cousin's family on my father's side is coming today to watch KC? They traveled all the way from Win-nemucca. Can you start him at pitcher, please, everyone in the family would love to see him pitch today?" yells KC's mom out toward the field in Pablo's direction so that everyone in the stands knows they have relatives in town.

Relatives attending the baseball game pose its own challenge to the starting lineup card for the coach. All Little League coaches want play-ers to do their best in front of friends and fami-ly. When grandma and grandpa are in town to watch a game, the pressure to perform well is ratcheted up a hundred notches. Coach Pablo must remain steadfast in his decisions to build the starting lineup based on the players that can give the team the best opportunity to suc-ceed.

The "professional wrestling battle royal" Brent's dad has grappled with this morning—between family relatives attending, player atti-tudes and readiness, and baseball strategy—produces the victor—baseball strategy. "This is the best starting lineup I can put on the field today, based on how we matchup against that Westside team," says Coach to his sunflower seed package. "I know what we can do against Westside. I've got players stacked in the best spot for success. Now all we need to do is execute!" Coach Pablo glances down one last time at his notebook:

The Question:

Eagles vs. Warriors pitching matchup, ability to bunt, steal bases, hit the opposite way, strength of the bottom of the order, staggering better hitters throughout the lineup, ability to catch a fly ball, pitch count limitations in little league, how each team's players performed over their most recent games—*can they handle the pressure of the Championship game, and are they prepared?*

The Answer:

Eagles should win today!

Coach Pablo feels satisfied that they are ready for the day's all-important competition. After a long morning of deliberations, which seem vaguely similar to a jury pondering the guilt or innocence of a defendant on trial, Brent's dad finishes his lukewarm coffee and scribbles down the Eagles starting lineup card with his lucky blue ink pen:

Batting First and Starting at Catcher
#1 Brent

Batting Second and Starting at Pitcher
#5 Jerald

Batting Third and Starting in Center Field
#20 Danny / Triple D

Batting Fourth and Starting at Shortstop
#19 KC

Batting Fifth and Starting at Third Base
#9 Todd / Turtle

Batting Sixth and Starting at First Base
#6 Mitchell / Milkshake

Batting Seventh and Starting in Left Field
#4 Dallas

Batting Eighth and Starting in Right Field
#23 Joey

Batting Ninth and Starting at Second Base
#99 Manny

On the Bench
#13 Reese, #34 Hector, #47 Donnie/Don Juan

Chapter 5

Sellout Crowd

"There it is, bud," Brent's father says to him. The family blue F-150 Ford truck carrying father and son makes the long, lazy, right-hand turn down the single lane dusty road towards the Lewis and Clark Baseball Complex. Brent's stomach is doing flip-flops. He can't contain his excitement. "I can't believe this day is finally here! I'm so jacked to play this game!"

Throughout the remainder of the morning, Little League players, coaches, parents, relatives, children, and animals will make the trek down the dusty road to the ball diamond. The early morning peace and tranquility that the doves and quails, gophers, and squirrels have been enjoying at the Lewis and Clark Ballpark will soon be replaced with obnoxious, screeching barbarians. Spectators begin jockeying for the perfect spot to plant their lawn chair to watch the action around Field 5. The Oklahoma Land Rush of 1889 was tame in comparison to fans staking their claim to the best spot to watch today's Championship game.

Pickup trucks and minivans park backwards in various spots along the entire outfield fence. Tailgates and hatchbacks begin dropping down like well-wishers heaving pennies into a fountain at the mall. Similar to a Civil War reenactment scene, an army of popup tents sprout up along the left and right field foul lines.

Ice chests, charcoal barbeques, Traeger cooker-smokers, lawn chairs, and umbrellas grow like weeds in an abandoned yard. Parents, kids, and fans of all ages mill around the baseball complex with enough pure raw nervous energy to power all the lights at Fenway Park in Boston for the 82-game regular season Red Sox schedule.

"How long 'til game time?" a couple of kids ask their mom.

"It will be awhile, Honey. Do you want some apple slices or gum?" she replies.

"No, thanks! Can I have ten bucks instead, to get a snow cone, corn dog, hot dog, chips, pop-corn, and..." comes a hopeful voice from the little one in the group.

The perturbed mother cuts the child off. "Ten dollars? NO! Get a foul ball during the game and take it to the Snack Shack. They will give you a snow cone in exchange for the ball. And, no, you cannot have all that junk food. Here is a dollar. You can get a juice box."

A boom box comes to life with the discovery of an electrical outlet plug underneath the right field scoreboard. The ballpark now bumps along to Snoop Dogg, Dr. Dre, and Vanilla Ice, as the cars thicken up on the gravel parking lot.

All possible spaces for trucks and tents around Field 5 are filling up fast. Field 5 at the Lewis and Clark Baseball Complex completes its metamorphosis from sleepy baseball park to a rowdy National Football League professional football-type tailgate.

Eerily similar to an Oakland Raiders parking lot prior to a Sunday football game, cars and trucks are parked in all directions, wedged into the smallest of spaces. The music, food, and atmosphere could easily be confused with a Raider Nation event.

"Man, I am so nervous. Harold, hand me one of those 'psst goes the sound of a 12-ounce beer can of liquid courage'." One eager dad slyly dips into his concealed ice chest to give another dad on the team an adult beverage.

"Harold, do you remember last year's 10-year-old Championship game?" asks the freshly imbibed friend.

"Kind of, sort of, wasn't that the game the kid ran over the catcher? I mean, just blew him up and both benches cleared? A big brawl started with punches coming from every direction and the cops had to come break it up?" says Harold.

"Something like that. So the game is tied in the bottom of the sixth inning and a kid is on second base. A ball is hit to left field and then the third base coach starts frantically waving the kid around third base to try and score the winning run. The kid on second gets about three feet in front of home plate and slides, knees first, into the catcher," says the beer-toting dad.

"What! Knees first, I don't remember that!" says Harold.

"Yeah, the kid barrels into home plate, knees first, just as the ball is coming in from left field. The left fielder has a heck of an arm and guns it towards home plate. It's a perfect throw. Well, the catcher gets the ball on one bounce from the outfielder and the kid from second is sliding into home on his knees like some Flash Dance movie move and ends up knocking the catcher off balance. The umpire calls 'safe', and the game should be over," extols the chuckling dad.

"Okay, now I remember. Didn't the coaches and fans from the losing team run onto the field?" says Harold.

"You got it—and the catcher runs into the opposing team's dugout trying to punch the lights out of the runner. The catcher is stopped by the winning team's manager. *However*, when the daddy-coach looks up from grabbing the catcher, there are three opposing coaches, two moms, and the League President all in his face, ready to punch him! What's funny is you can hear the catcher crying and yelling at the same time about how he doesn't play baseball to get run over and it's just a game, blah-blah-blah. There is no way that catcher could have been hurt! The kid sliding into home on his knees weighed about fifty pounds. It was crazy!" continues the dad, as he takes another sip from his can.

"Everyone lost their minds, right?" remembers Harold.

"Yup. So, the League President is the dad of the catcher. He demands the runner be called out for not sliding. The home plate umpire says he did slide—just knees first. Parents are on the field yelling at the umpire. The League President is yelling at everyone. It's a scream fest straight out of wrestle mania. Anyway, the League President ends up throwing the umpire out of the game! Can you believe it? He throws the umpire out of the game! The field umpire is his son, so he gets tossed out, as well."

"Then the League President calls in two new volunteers to umpire the game. He says the run does not count, the game is still tied, and play will resume when the new umpires get to the field," explains the storyteller dad.

"Then the team, that just thought they won, lost their minds and started yelling, right?" says Harold.

"The cops were called, and it's the biggest mess I've ever seen at a youth sporting event!" says the fan, now with his empty beer in hand.

"Wait 'til later today. I think you could have a new first place winner, the way these teams and fans do not like each other," concludes Harold.

Coach Pablo and the Westside Warriors coach make eye contact in the parking lot as they head toward Field 5.

"I just don't like that manager, Brent. He makes me so angry I can't see straight," says Pablo to his son. "Westside and Eastside don't see eye to eye. It's not a friendly rivalry between the two teams. It's an old-fashioned slugfest. Each side is mad at the other, and neither group can remember what started the feud."

The baseball games played between the foul lines have been close, entertaining, and well managed.

A dark red cloud of bad blood, however, hovers over all Warriors and Eagles games. This Saturday afternoon in early June will be no different—the forecast is for a close game played between the boys, with a downpour of heckling from irate spectators, mixed with uncontrollable hatred for 'BLUE'.

BLUE is also known as—"The Umpire."

The pickup truck regatta parked in left field at Field 5 spots a volunteer umpire in the back of his Prius, putting on his shin guards, chest protector, protective cup, and baby blue umpire shirt.

"Hey, BLUE, did you bring your glasses today?" yells an obnoxious spectator, lounging on the tailgate of his 1977 Chevy LUV pickup truck to the volunteer dad umpire.

The first pitch hasn't even been thrown yet in today's ballgame played between 12-year olds. Brent can see and hear the exchange be-

tween the fans and the umpire behind the left
field fence.

"Yeah, you suck, man!" chimes his buddy,
resting on the tailgate of the small rusted
pickup truck.

A primal urge, which defies logic, envelops
parents, fans, coaches, and even 12-year-old
ballplayers, all with the objective to scream
their heads off at umpires. The fact that umpires are 100% volunteers who give of their time
freely makes no difference to the screaming
fans.

Yelling, screaming, and cruel behavior toward umpires is a sad, pathetic part of youth
baseball.

The crowd at the Lewis and Clark Baseball
Complex does not have to pay for their tickets to
watch today's Championship game action. But
that does not stop them from behaving like they
paid $1,000 for a precious front row leather seat
at Yankee Stadium, thus entitling them to verbally assault the umpires.

"Hey, Coach," says Brent to the Eastside
Eagles assistant coach.

"Yeah, kiddo?"

"Why are those guys giving the umpire such a bad time even before the game starts?" asks Brent.

The Eastside assistant coach looks at Brent in surprise and nods, showing he understands Brent's question. "You'd think life and death rest with each call from the umpires, according to this delusional bunch of narcissists," he says.

"You know, those dads that umpire the game aren't that bad, they're actually pretty nice. I get to talk with them during the game while I'm catching. Most of them are really funny. We crack jokes during the game. It's pretty cool," Brent admits to his assistant coach.

Umpires' ball and strike judgment calls behind home plate serve the youth baseball crowd like gladiators in the Colosseum of Rome. Once the red meat (also labeled outrage) begins to be eaten in the lion's den, it does not matter who gets the brunt of the vicious attacks from the crowd. Coaches and young kid ballplayers are equal opportunity targets for the sellout crowd's venom.

Each perceived bad call from the volunteer umpire serves up more bloodthirsty opportunities for outrage from the violent fans.

Fans in the stands 30 feet from the action falsely believe they have a perfect vantage point to provide commentary on the game. In their delusional minds, the bleachers obviously have *no bad seats or obstructed views*. Spectators think they see every pitched ball with *perfect eyesight*.

Umpires positioned directly behind home plate, squarely in front of the pitcher and with the batter a mere two feet from the action, serve as the WORST vantage point to call balls and strikes, according to the sellout crowd of heathens.

"Coach, I'm going over there and tell those guys to give the umps a break. Umps are not bad guys. They need to forgive them for bad calls. They are just trying to do their best," says Brent.

Umpiring is a difficult job with numerous split-second decisions. The volunteer umpires are given two half-day training sessions, are handed the 100 page rulebook, and told to 'Have fun' umpiring youth baseball games. Volunteer umpires can and do miss calls on the field during baseball games. Chalk it up to lack of training. Missed calls have been and will be a part of baseball. The human element of volunteer umpires is part of the game. Youth baseball society, however, wants instant revenge for any outrageous call that goes against *their* team.

"Brent, it's best not to get involved between those angry guys and the umpire... just ignore it. Stay focused on yourself, and get prepared for the game today," advises the assistant coach.

"I heard those guys at a game earlier this year in the outfield. They don't even know the rules or how come they are mad at the umpires," Brent replies crossly.

The rules of baseball seem not to get in the way of a good opportunity to display hatred from the stands. A batter swings at the ball and misses. However, the ball travels into the body of the batter. The crowd yells, "It hit him you, blind bat, he should go to first base!" Not according to the rules of baseball, which the umpire has studied, and the crowd has not. The correct call is a strike on the batter.

"Brent, *last time*, let it go. You can't do anything about it. It's not your fight! Now stay focused on your job," the coach sternly warns him.

"Alright, but those guys need to forgive the umpires. It's just silly to yell at them!" insists Brent.

The sellout crowd circling Field 5 continue their pre-game preparations for the day's action. The crowd's main goal for the contest is to distract a 12-year-old on the pitching mound, in the field, or at home plate, by any means possible to gain the advantage for *their* team.

The traditional duck blind of shooting insults once reserved in the bleachers behind home plate has been replaced with an all-over-the-field yelling strategy. Hecklers are strategically located as close to the action as possible for maximum insult range.

"You been working on any new material for the game today?" says a dad, reclining in his lawn chair next to his friend.

"Yeah, check this out. I'm going to yell everyone hits today! He's got nothing! Everyone hits this pitcher today when that Jerald kid takes the mound!" says his buddy, as he proudly thumps his shirt that reads **#1 Warrior Fan & My Son Is An All-Star And Yours Is Not.**

His wife, the mom of a benchwarmer on the Westside Warriors, chimes in, "I'm going to start yelling 'Whoo! Whoo! Whoo!' from the very first pitch of the baseball game today."

The sellout crowd is dedicated to its job (more seriously than to their 9 AM to 5 PM weekday employment) of intimidating and influencing the outcome of the day's baseball game.

Before the teams take the field for warm ups, the crowd is busy looking for little rocks to put into their empty water bottles. The crowd will use the water bottles filled with tiny rocks to shake when the opposing pitcher is on the mound. The ruckus created by the rock-filled water bottles feels familiar to thunder sticks and cow bells that are shaken at college football and professional basketball games. Even paid professional athletes have a difficult time tuning out the noise while trying to stay focused on their jobs.

Rocks in bottles are not the only annoying tools at the sellout crowd's disposal. CHANTS, lots of various bloodcurdling CHANTS, are uttered during the entire contest.

"That lady on the Westside team that wears that stupid **"#1 Warrior Fan & My Son Is An All-Star And Yours Is Not"** tank top made me so mad when she came your way last time and yelled, 'my precious little buddy boo,' and 'I love you, my precious little buddy boo,' and 'I'm proud of you, my precious little buddy boo,' and 'it's okay, my precious little buddy boo,' in the last game we played them. If she does it *again* today, I'm not going to control my anger. I will find her and take care of her!" threatens Donnie's mom, Megyn.

The slogans and chants with choreographed hand gestures once reserved for softball and European futbol fans is now commonplace throughout 12-year-old baseball games at the Lewis and Clark ballpark.

"Hey, Mom, we have been practicing our chants. Want to hear them?" beg a couple of younger brothers of the Westside Warriors players.

"Not now, Honey," says the distracted mom.

Ignoring her answer, the boys start to sing, "Okay, here we go, We Believe That We Will Win (repeat 1,000 times), B. A. T. T. attle Battle baby battle, 3 & 2 Count on the Batter: 3-2 What's ya gonna do? Rip It! Rip It!, Good Eye, Good Eye, G Double O, D, E, Y. Good Eye, Who Let the Dogs Out! Whoot Whoot, You Got A Piece of It, Now We Want All of It!"

"Stop!" pleads the mom.

"But these are our best ones!" giggle the boys. "Rolling Rolling Rolling, this Pitcher is Going Bowling, The Cops are Coming, The Cops are Coming, We Stole A Base, Don't You Know, Can't You Guess? We are the Best!"

"That's it! Get out of here!" yells the mom.

The boys take off running away from the adults, singing as loud as they can, "Hit 'em high, hit 'em low, hit 'em outta Idaho!"

Across town, the county sheriff checks in for the day's shift. He glances at his patrol schedule and sees:

Lewis and Clark Baseball Complex Championship Saturday. Drive around parking lot at least four times from 8:00 AM to 5:00 PM and BE ALERT.

The sheriff remembers very well his encounters with angry parents over the years at the baseball fields. "I still can't believe I booked into custody a grown man, 45 years of age, who was coaching in the first base box and got directly in the face of a volunteer high school field umpire, pushing his finger so hard into the kid he drew blood. That coach yelled his head off and threatens the kid umpire with bodily harm for missing a foul ball call over the first base bag. Just nuts!" grumbles the sheriff to his deputy.

"Not as bad as I witnessed, sitting in the parking lot with the coach. He let loose a string of profanities that would make Chris Rock blush to a dad umpire. Then the umpire yelled, 'That's it, Coach! Meet me in the parking lot after the game! We will settle this like men!'" the deputy tells the sheriff, shaking his head.

The Little League Championship game played between the Westside Warriors and Eastside Eagles will be a target-rich environment for anger and hatred, as they goad obscene behavior by adults who have lost their way.

"Time for my patrol. I'm off to the Lewis and Clark Ballpark. Pray nothing happens this championship weekend!" As he leaves, the sheriff salutes the American and Vietnam P.O.W. flags flying outside the police station.

Chapter 6

Under the Lights

"Please rise and remove your caps. To honor America with the singing of our National Anthem, please welcome Pam Lindsey!" announces the President of Lewis and Clark Baseball Complex to a noisy Championship day crowd.

"Hey, I know that girl! Her brother hit a home run in last year's Championship game over the left field fence that landed in that farmer's field!" says a sibling of one of the Eastside Eagles team to another kid watching the Westside Warriors team from the stands.

"Yeah, I remember! The ball hit that farmer's goat right in the butt! It was awesome," whispers the giggly kid to his friendly rival.

"You boys, knock it off, and remove your hats. Be respectful. Everyone knows her brother died this spring in that car accident with her father. I don't know how she is able to sing the National Anthem. I would be a wreck," says the Westside boy's mother.

Voice quivering, Pam takes the handheld microphone, wipes away a couple of tears, and begins to sing.

> "O say, can you see, by the dawn's early light,
> What so proudly we hailed at the twilight's last gleaming?
> Whose broad stripes and bright stars, through the perilous fight,
> O'er the ramparts we watched, were so gallantly streaming?
> And the rocket's red glare, the bombs bursting in air,
> Gave proof through the night that our flag was still there.
> O say, does that star spangled banner yet wave—

O'er the land of the free, and the home of the brave?

On the shore dimly seen through the mists of the deep.
Where the foe's haughty host in dread silence reposes,
What is that which the breeze, o'er the towering steep,
As it fitfully blows, half conceals, half discloses?
Now it catches the gleam of the morning's first beam,
In full glory reflected now shines in the stream:
'Tis the Star-Spangled Banner! O long may it wave
O'er the land of the free and the home of the brave.

And where is that band who so vauntingly swore
That the havoc of war and the battle's confusion
A home and a country should leave us no more?

Their blood has washed out their
foul footsteps' pollution.
　No refuge could save the hireling
and slave
　From the terror of flight, or the
gloom of the grave:
　And the Star-Spangled Banner,
in triumph doth wave
　O'er the land of the free and the
home of the brave.

　O thus be it ever when freemen
shall stand
　Between their loved homes and
the war's desolation!
　Blest with vict'ry and peace, may
the Heaven-rescued land
　Praise the Power that hath made
and preserved us a nation.
　Then conquer we must when our
cause it is just—
　And this be our motto: "In God is
our Trust."
　And the Star-Spangled Banner in
triumph shall wave
　O'er the land of the free and the
home of the brave!"

Pam finishes the song with a strong voice and a wry smile and points her index fingers up to the heavens, in memory of her older brother who died when their father accidentally ran over the boy with their family car. Pam hands the microphone back to the President of the Lewis and Clark Baseball Complex. She walks toward her father, past the ball players who are waiting for the game to start outside their respective dugouts. Her dad is located just on the other side of the fence behind home plate. The sellout crowd is eerily silent, as if attending a funeral.

"That was beautiful, Pumpkin," says Pam's dad quietly, knowing how Pam has struggled to be able to sing since her brother's death.

"Thank you. I love you, Dad, and I forgive you for the car accident," Pam says, with a mist of tears brimming in her eyes.

Standing near home plate, waiting on his turn in the opening day ceremony processional, Brent can see and hear the entire exchange between father and daughter.

The two energetic boys, who were earlier told to hush, begin whistling and clapping their

hands in approval of the girl's outstanding singing performance.

Now encouraged, the stunned crowd joins
the boys in joyous applause. The crowd remains
standing as the rolling thunder of approval and
sympathy ripples over the field like a pebble hitting a mountain lake.

Wiping tears away from his eyes, the President of the Lewis and Clark Sports Complex
takes the microphone back from Pam. "Throwing out the ceremonial first pitch for today's
Championship game is Milo Rowell, a veteran of
the Iraq War and hometown hero!" the President announces with a cracking voice.

The Lewis and Clark Baseball Complex
President is extremely nervous, fumbling over
his 3x5 flash cards that contain today's agenda
and script for the Championship Day festivities.

Milo lost the use of his right arm in the war,
diving on an improvised exploding device to pro-
tect his unit from harm. Milo grew up on the
Lewis and Clark baseball fields, and still holds
the record for most strikeouts with 15 K's in an
11-year-old baseball game. The crowd remains
standing, showering him with applause for his

bravery. A brief reminder that the crowd is blessed to live in a free country where the game of baseball is allowed to be played by young boys.

"Boy, it feels great to be back on the mound!" Milo shouts to Brent over the loud clapping and whistling, as he lobs the ball left-handed into home plate. Brent is the honorary catcher for the ceremonial first pitch from Milo.

"That was great. Nice lefty knuckleball, Mr. Rowell!" Brent smiles, handing the brand new baseball back to Milo. Then his voice lowers. "Can I ask you something?" Brent whispers to Milo.

"Yeah, go ahead and ask anything. We Little League players stick together," says Milo, giving him a friendly wink.

"How come you are happy? If I lost my arm I would be angry at those guys in Iraq that took it. I would be mad all the time," Brent asks softly.

Milo puts his left arm around Brent, "I'm thankful I'm alive *and* I get to live in Idaho. I'm blessed to have a left arm that works enough to throw out the first pitch today. I forgave those guys I was fighting against a long time ago. I don't carry hatred around—it's too heavy! If other people see my not having an arm as a problem, well, that's *their* problem!" Milo answers without hesitation.

Brent nods, but he isn't done thinking about what he has just heard.

"Have a great game today, buddy. Give it your best effort. And remember, life is too short to carry around hatred!" finishes Milo.

Brent and Milo left-hand fist bump each other and share a baseball player's smile together as they walk off the field. The Championship day ceremonies are coming to a close and it's just about game time.

Unlike the beauty of a caterpillar turning into a butterfly, the fanatical bleachers and spectators in foul territory around the park will begin to morph into a raging fever of evil. The selfless service to others so elegantly displayed by Pam and Milo will be instantly forgotten. The light switch of serving others will be switched to pride in a matter of moments. The crowd will replace the atmosphere of sacrifice with a fleshly self-centered mantra full of 'look at me and see what *my* kid can do on the field.' Fans will use umpires and managers as their excuse if their child does not perform well. "They are all out to get me, and the coach has it in for my son," will be the crowd's reaction to poor play.

While the fans are itching for the game to start, the two volunteer dad umpires begin the pre-game safety check ritual. The umpires double-check the safety list from behind third base. The umpires will each walk the entire field, looking for any possible safety issues. They will inspect the outfield fence for defects, and check for holes in the field. They will carefully pick up each of the player's bats, looking for dents. They inspect each player's batting helmet for cracks, and will spread out the catcher's gear to make sure there is a throat guard and chest protector tail to cover the catcher's lower extremities. "Safety first" is the guiding light.

Finally, both umpires prepare the baseballs for use in the game by rubbing them down with a little dirt while talking to each other about one another's responsibility for the game. They review the rules and where they will be positioned on the field for calls. They will try their best to work as a team today, and to avoid the

howls from fans positioned all around the diamond.

"Jerald and Brent, you guys are captains today. Head towards the plate." Coach Pablo sees
they are ready.

The Westside Warriors and Eastside Eagles
teams each send player captains for today's
Championship game to home plate to meet with
the umpires. And with the selection of team captains, the chirping from the stands shoots off
like fireworks celebrating the Fourth of July.

"It's always the stupid coach's kid that gets
to be the captain!" shouts a parent while checking major league baseball scores on his iPhone.

"Congratulations, guys, on making it to the
Championship game," says the home plate umpire. "Your teams are to be commended on a
great season. Let's have fun today. We want to
make sure you guys practice safety at all times.
No phitens choker-chains can be worn around
your neck, no long-sleeve white undershirts for
pitchers, and no on-deck batter can be outside
the dugout. If a player has to go to the bath-
room, Coaches, please call time so we can get a
volunteer to escort them to the restroom. Hustle

on and off the field as quickly as possible. Pitchers get one minute to warm up between innings. No coaches can warm up the pitcher, only ball players. All lineup changes must be brought to me first, do not go to the scorekeeper. Come to me first, got it? Any questions? No? Good! Then shake hands," the umpire finishes his scholarly lecture.

"Okay, Eagles, call the coin in the air," the home plate umpire begins.

"Heads!" calls Brent.

"It is heads," the umpire nods towards Brent.

"We want to be home!" Brent declares enthusiastically, even before the umpire can ask him if Eastside wants to be the home or visiting team.

"Boys, have a good game, and best of luck to each of your teams. Head back to your dugouts. Eastside, take the field. Your pitcher has one minute to warm up," instructs the home plate umpire in the most authoritative tone he can muster. The umpire is going to need all of his command and control abilities for the game, or the crowd will eat him alive like a swarm of mosquitoes at dusk.

"Would you look at that, the San Francisco Giants are losing to the Colorado Rockies, what a joke!" the parent checking scores on his iPhone says out loud to himself. Startled to see Eastside taking the field, he chimes in, "Lucky they are the home team. Westside must have lost the coin flip."

The Eastside Eagles gather in front of the third base dugout with eye black smeared onto their faces, and with their caps, gloves, and sunglasses at the ready.

"Alright, boys, remember to play with *no fear* today. Give 100% energy and effort and the Championship game is yours for the taking. EAGLES, on three!"

"One, two, three, EAGLES!" shout the 12 players in unison.

The starting nine ball players jump over the third base foul line chalk, and fly out to their positions.

Reese runs along foul territory toward left field to warm up Dallas, the left fielder. Donnie and Hector slowly walk back into the dugout. Each player grabs a clipboard and golf pencil as they prepare to tally each of Jerald's pitches against the Westside Warriors batters from the dugout bench. The boys are assigned the job of charting pitches. It's boring, but extremely important, to make sure pitch count rules are strictly followed.

The Eagles looked sharp in drills, and now it's carried over to the one-minute warmup offered during Jerald's pitches. With the exception of KC at shortstop, who has to tie his shoe for the third time today, the team appears ready and focused.

"Okay, Catcher, two more," the home plate umpire says to Brent.

"Balls in, coming down!" yells Brent to the Eagles players positioned in the field.

Brent takes the eighth warm up pitch from Jerald, and throws it as if it were on a frozen rope to Manny at second base. Manny misses the ball and it gets past KC who is supposed to back up the catcher's throw. Danny in center field isn't paying attention and the ball gets by him, as well.

"Let's go! Pick it up! Come on!" yells the coaching staff and three hundred not-so-encouraging fans of the Eagles.

"Not a great way to start," says Coach Pablo to himself. Hatred nips at Coach Pablo's heels. "We can't have those stupid mistakes. We haven't even started the game yet! Hector, throw me that bag of sunflower seeds now," growls the coach.

"PLAY!" screams the home plate umpire to Jerald on the mound.

Butler, Gannon, and Kylan—the pitcher, catcher, and shortstop—lead off the batting order for the Warriors. The three players combined for ten hits in the previous matchup with the Eagles. The Eagles' only regular season loss on the year was at the hands of the Warriors.

Jerald's first pitch of the Championship game is a fastball. Butler greets the first pitch with a solid swing, and the ball careens off the top of the fence in straight away centerfield.

Butler cruises into second base with a leadoff double.

"It's alright, Triple D! Remember, your first step is always backward on a fly ball!" yells Coach Pablo toward Danny, the centerfielder. "Jerald, you will be fine. Just keep throwing strikes, and remember to move the ball around," Coach Pablo instructs, sitting on his padded ball bucket inside the third base dugout.

Gannon is the second batter in the order for the Westside Warriors. He receives two quick strikes from Jerald. The no ball and two strikes offering from Jerald to Gannon is a weakly hit grounder toward Manny at second base. Manny charges the ball with his glove in the dirt, catches the ball cleanly, and throws the ball on target to Milkshake (Mitchell) at first base for the out.

Butler takes third base on the play.

"Batting third for the Warriors is Kylan!" calls the announcer over the loud speakers.

Kylan hits the first pitch offered by Jerald. It's a routine ground ball to Milkshake at first base. Milkshake is not ready for the hit, and the baseball goes right between his legs, bounding into right field.

"I wish Milkshake would have barfed all over himself at practice," thinks Jerald as he watches Joey in right field pick up the baseball and throw it to KC standing on second base.

Butler scores the first run of the Championship game for the Warriors. Milkshake Mitchell is the first player to cry in the Championship game. The Eagles home scorekeeper gives Mitchell an error on the ground ball.

The Warrior's electronic scorekeeper credits Kylan with a hit. The scorekeeper is Kylan's mom Bernice. She thinks it was a hard hit ball and a tough play for the first baseman. As a stats bonus, the scoring play will increase Kylan's batting average and runs batted in total.

"Flush it, Jerald!" yells Coach Pablo from the third base dugout to the pitcher's mound. "Brent, son, keep the target low for Jerald so we can get the batter to hit another ground ball, right now!" he screams as he gets up from his seated position on the lid of the baseball bucket.

Jerald slowly regains his composure and searches deep down to grasp some self-control. He offers the number four batter on the Warriors a nasty change-up pitch, and the batter hits a ground ball to KC.

The Eagles shortstop effortlessly scoops up the ball and flips it to Manny who is covering second base. Manny easily catches the ball and then turns and throws the ball to Mitchell at first base. Milkshake catches the ball thrown from Manny coming in from second base for the double play.

All the scorekeepers mark down 6-4-3 on the play, resulting in an inning-ending double play for the Eagles.

Teams	1	2	3	4	5	6
WARRIORS	1					
EAGLES						

Before Brent steps into the batter's box to begin the home half of the first inning, he checks the signs from the third base coach, his dad Pablo. Coach Pablo brushes his hands on his hat then down his arms and across his uniform. He claps his hands and yells at Brent, "Find a way to get on first base, be a leadoff hitter!" Brent's heart is pounding out of his chest. His nerves are racing like a Kentucky Derby three-year-old thoroughbred racehorse coming down the last furlong toward the finish line.

Brent sees the sign from his dad is to get a bunt for a base hit. The pitch comes right down the middle, and he bunts the ball down the third base line where no one can get the ball. He executes the bunt to perfection. Brent arrives at first base with an infield single.

The Warriors manager elected to start Butler in the Championship game. A solid baseball move, given Butler was credited with the win the last time the two teams played.

"Now, batting second for the Eagles is the pitcher Jerald!" comes over the loudspeakers.

The first pitch to Jerald from Butler, the Warriors hurler, is a curveball that bounces in the dirt right in front of home plate. Brent sees the ball in the dirt and takes off from first base at lightning speed for second base. The throw from Gannon, the Warriors catcher, is not in time, and Brent has stolen second base! The Eagles dugout erupts in joy with high fives being slapped in all directions.

Muffled applause, mimicking a gallery golf clap seen at Professional Golfers Association tournaments, emanates from the Eastside Eagles stands for the coach's kid.

Jerald has worked the count to 3 balls and 2 strikes. The next pitch from Butler is whacked into the gap between right field and center field, easily scoring Brent from second base. "Great hit, Jerald!" yells Milkshake from the dugout toward first base where Jerald is camped out.

"YES!" yells Coach Pablo with clinched fist pumping away in the third base coach's box.

The game announcer clicks on the microphone, "Danny, the Number 3 batter for the Eagles, is up to bat!"

Before putting both neon yellow cleats into the batters' box, Danny checks with Coach Pablo to see if there is a sign. He sees Coach put two hands on his knees, which means take the first pitch, no matter what.

"Two hands on knees. Don't swing, no mat-
ter what!" screams Danny to himself.

Danny takes the pitch thrown from Butler,
and Jerald dashes for second base, as Gannon
catches the ball behind home plate. Gannon's
throw to second base is not in time, and Jerald
has a stolen the base. The Eagles stands go crazy with the play and the dugout is on fire with
teammates chest bumping each other in unbridled enthusiasm.

Danny hits the next pitch offered by Butler
off the pitcher's leg, which rebounds over toward
Kylan at shortstop. He picks up the loose ball
and throws to first base in time to get Danny.
Jerald cannot advance from second base on the
ricochet.

"Butler, you okay?" yells the Warriors manager seated upon his padded ball bucket along
the first base dugout. A throbbing pain similar
to hitting your finger with a hammer emanates
from Butler's shinbone where the ball off Danny's bat hit him.

"Man, that hurts! That clown tried to hit me
on purpose when he swung at my pitch," complains Butler to his coach on the bucket. Then,

eyeing KC, Butler mumbles, "If that's the way you want to play, then take *this*." Butler hits KC with his first pitch. KC, the shortstop and number four batter for the Eagles, takes the first pitch offered by Butler squarely in the middle of his back. He knows all too well how much it hurts, having been hit nine times during the season.

"Charge the mound, KC!" yells Donnie from the Eagles' dugout bench.

"Relax, Donnie. KC gets first base. Just forget about Butler, and let's score some more runs," Brent urges Don Juan Donnie who is sitting next to him on the bench.

Anger and hatred team up just at the right time to produce a double whammy of evil aimed at Brent. "You're a wimp, Brent! KC needs to go out to the mound and punch his lights out! We don't need any forgive-and-forget garbage!" screams an angry and frustrated Donnie.

All patrons surrounding Field 5 come to a fever pitch that resembles the Boston Symphony Orchestra hitting the climax of a Beethoven's Symphony Number 7. The Eastside Eagles parents are in full throat, with fists in the air, yelling at Warrior parents that Butler hit KC on purpose. Horns blaring from trucks behind the centerfield wall begin to go off like a 21-gun salute at a military memorial.

"*TIME!*" yells the home plate umpire.

"Both Managers, get off your ball buckets, and get to home plate, right *NOW!*" screams the volunteer home plate umpire. Coach Pablo and the Warriors manager sheepishly approach home plate. "Gentlemen, tell your boys to knock it off right now! I know the past history between your ball clubs. This isn't a major league baseball game. We will not have pitchers throwing at batters! Period," orders the umpire.

The President of the Lewis and Clark Baseball Complex opens his phone and searches his contacts for the phone number of the county sheriff.

"But he didn't... ," the Warrior coach starts to say, but before he can finish his sentence, the home plate umpire turns his back on both managers.

"Play!" says the umpire as he crouches down behind Gannon, the Warriors catcher.

The sellout crowd has not slowed down one bit in their high octane screaming. Butler takes his place on the pitcher's mound. He looks around the entire ballpark in amazement at the vile and vicious language coming from all parents attending the game. The Warriors pitcher is obviously rattled by the angry sellout crowd, the Eagles dugout, and the stern warning he received from the umpire not to throw at any more batters.

"Now batting, the Number 5 hitter, Todd!" says the announcer, noticing that the noise from the stadium is so loud no one hears the Eagles player announcement.

Todd receives four straight balls that are nowhere near the strike zone.

"Great job, Turtle! Way to earn that base on balls!" yells Brent to Todd as he slowly, very slowly, walks toward first base.

The bases are now full of Eastside Eagles players. Milkshake is the next batter up for the Eagles. He doesn't look toward third base for a sign from his coach. Milkshake jumps right into the batter's box with both feet. He swings wildly at the first two pitches over his head offered by

Butler. The third pitch is outside and low, but the umpire calls the pitch a strike for the second out of the inning.

"You have got to be kidding me, BLUE, that's horrible!" The catcalls ring out from the Eagles fans. Milkshake cries again, as he walks back to the dugout. His head is down and the bat is dragging behind him in the red clay diamond dust dirt of Field 5.

The Eagles bench and stands continue to yell out in disbelief at the called third strike on Milkshake.

With two down, the bases still loaded, and Dallas, the seventh batter in the lineup, at the plate, Coach Pablo pleads for a big hit. "Come on, Dallas, focus!"

We need you to get a hit, big guy!" Coach Pablo calls from the third base coach's box.

Unfortunately for the Eagles faithful fans, Dallas hits the first pitch thrown by Butler to the Warriors third baseman, who gently steps on his base to get the third out of the inning.

Teams	1	2	3	4	5	6
WARRIORS	1					
EAGLES	1					

The top of the second inning begins with a ball hit to center field that Triple D Danny is late to chase down. The ball hits the outfield turf right in front of him and caroms off a sprinkler over his head all the way to the centerfield fence 250 feet away from home plate. The Warriors batter goes all the way to third base on the play.

Jerald's very next pitch is off Brent's catcher's glove and rolls past him all the way to the backstop. The runner from third base breaks for home plate in an attempt to steal home and score the go-ahead run.

Jerald races from the pitcher's mound to home plate in hopes of getting the runner, while at the same time yelling to Brent, "The runner is coming! The runner is coming!" Brent picks up the baseball resting against the backstop with his bare hand, and turns toward home plate. He takes three large steps and dives at home plate, like a 50-meter speed swimmer starting an Olympic Gold Medal swimming race. Brent and the base runner trying to score from third base arrive just in front of home plate at the same time.

"The runner is OUT!" yells the home plate umpire. Brent had applied the tag before the runner could reach home plate for the first out of the inning.

Now it's the Warriors fans' turn to go insane, with rude and crude insults for the home plate umpire. "He missed the tag! He missed the tag!" "He was safe! You cheater!" "You idiot!" rings out rudely from the bleachers and foul territory planted with Warriors fans.

Jerald is relieved to get the out at home plate.

"Funny how the Warriors think you are terrible, now," Brent laughs behind his catcher's mask to the home plate umpire.

Jerald loses his concentration and walks the next Warrior batter on four pitches. After taking a deep breath and regaining his self-control,

Jerald strikes out the next two hitters, to end the top of the second.

Teams	1	2	3	4	5	6
WARRIORS	1	0				
EAGLES	1					

"Leading off the bottom of the second inning for the Eagles, Number 23, right fielder, Joey!" the game announcer shouts to the sellout crowd. Joey opens up the bottom of the second inning with a single to left field.

On the very next pitch from Butler, Joey steals second base. Joey's dad erupts. "Did you see my son steal second base! He's the fastest player in all of Idaho!" yells Joey's dad to every Eagles fan in the bleachers.

Manny, the Number 9 hitter in the Eagles batting lineup, is next up to the plate. Manny swings and misses the first two pitches offered by Butler. He watches the next two pitches miss the strike zone for a count of 2 balls and 2 strikes. With his eyes definitely closed, Manny swings as hard as he can at the next pitch from

Butler. Manny hits a rocket off Butler. The ball travels right between the pitcher's legs and directly over the second base bag. Joey was standing on second base, and the ball hit by Manny struck him directly in the thigh.

"The runner on second base is OUT!" screams the umpire in the field. "One out in the inning!"

Like a sudden breeze on a spring day, anger wafts throughout the stands. "The kid was standing on second base, Ump, when the ball hit him! He's not out, he's safe, you blind bat!" yells a mom from the Eagles' side of the bleachers.

The field umpire shakes his head after hearing the mom in the stands. The volunteer field umpire gathers himself, and in the most disgusted tone he can muster, yells, "The base is not a safe haven, and the ball clearly hit the runner resulting in an *out*. Sit down before I throw you out of the game for being a distraction!"

The Eagles coaches and fans from all corners of the sports complex react to the umpire's words with boos and shouting, telling the ump to focus on the game, not the fans. The umpire balance beam of keeping the game under control is tilting toward a call to police for assistance.

Next, Brent is up at bat for Eastside. Butler is clearly rattled again on the mound from all the yelling, and cannot find the strike zone. He walks Brent on four pitches. Brent drops his bat at home plate and sprints to first base, as if shot out of a cannon.

Jerald follows Brent in the batting order and smashes the second pitch offered by Butler into centerfield. The Warriors centerfield makes a great one-handed, over-the-shoulder running catch for the second out of the inning.

Manny, who was on second base after the walk to Brent, stands on second base as the centerfield makes the incredible catch for the out! Manny tags up from second base and tries to advance to third base, but is barely thrown out on the bang-bang play, for the third out of the inning. More yelling and screaming come from the stands as the close play at third base did not go the Eagles' way.

The Eagles fail to score a run in the home half of the second inning.

Teams	1	2	3	4	5	6
WARRIORS	1	0				
EAGLES	1	0				

The top of the third inning brings roster changes for the Eagles. Minimum play requirement rules state that every kid must play at least six consecutive defensive outs during the baseball game.

"Blue, I've got changes," says Coach Pablo to the home plate umpire.

"Alright, go ahead. What'cha got, Coach?" asks the ump.

"Reese #13 in for Jerald, Donnie #47 in for Mitchell, and Hector #34 in for Manny," replies Coach Pablo as he stares at his lineup card. Reese is now on the mound, pitching for the Eastside Eagles in the Championship game.

"Wow, look at this crowd. Wow, look at this field. Awesome, dude, can you believe it, this rocks, man," Reese says to Brent as he finishes his warmup pitches.

"Good luck, dude, remember to breathe, re-lax, and just throw strikes. You'll be fine," Brent encourages him. Reese, who replaced Jerald on the mound, is now ready to face the Warriors in the top of the third inning. Reese has great command of his fastball and is locating his pitches perfectly throughout the strike zone.

Baseball is a funny game, however; and But-ler, Gannon, and Kylan all reach base on infield singles. Not one hard hit ball off Reese's pitch-ing, and not one ball hit out of the infield, but the bases are still full of Warriors.

"Time!" yells Coach Pablo in the direction of the home plate umpire. Coach Pablo is still steamed by the close calls not going *his* way during the Championship.

"Everyone to the pitcher's mound, NOW!" yells the irate Coach. The Eagles third base-man, shortstop, second baseman, first baseman, and catcher sprint to the bump in the middle of the infield before Coach Pablo reaches the same destination. "Reese, bear down and throw hard, these guys can't touch your fastball. Brent, you catch everything and be a wall back there, so nothing gets past you. Todd, KC, Hector, and Donnie, play in on the grass, and if it's hit to

you, throw it home to Brent. Let's go!" barks
Coach Pablo.

Fear is a motivator. Reese turns his fear into a laser-like focus capable of splitting atoms.
Reese strikes out the next three Warriors batters he faces, ending the threat in the third
inning. Reese has kept the game tied at one run
apiece in the Championship game.

Teams	1	2	3	4	5	6
WARRIORS	1	0	0			
EAGLES	1	0				

The bottom of the third inning brings the
number 3, 4, and 5 hitters for the Eagles to the
plate—Danny, Todd and KC respectively.
"These three guys give us our best chance to put
some runs on the scoreboard," Coach Pablo
comments to his assistant coaches.

"They had a great week of practice, and
were really ripping the cover off the baseball
during batting practice," nods an assistant
coach.

137

The Eagles fans in the stands are hoping for a scoring rally from their boys. But not one of the 12-year-old sluggers can get on base. The Eagles go quietly in the home half of the third inning.

Teams	1	2	3	4	5	6
WARRIORS	1	0	0			
EAGLES	1	0	0			

"Catch, two more warmup pitches," says the home plate umpire to Brent.

" 'K," replies Brent.

"That's some cool catcher's gear you've got on," says the ump to Brent.

"Thanks, I put these blue and orange flame stickers on my mask all by myself," replies Brent, feeling pleased that the ump had noticed.

"That's sick, Yo! You'd the beast man, Yo! Truly wicked, Yo! You-za-the man Bro'heem's," replies the umpire in his most trying-to-be-a-cool-guy voice.

"You're hilarious, Blue," Brent chuckles to the umpire. Then to the Eagles shortstop, he yells, "Coming down, KC!" as he throws the ball to second base to complete the between-inning ritual of warming up the pitcher.

Reese is a little wild to start the fourth inning for the Eagles. He walks the leadoff batter on six pitches.

"Yo, B!" calls Jerald, using his personal nickname for Brent. "Get ready! I think this dude is going to try and steal second base on you!" he yells from the dugout toward catcher Brent who is ready for the pitch.

Reese delivers the pitch toward home plate, and the runner at first base heads toward second, like a sprinter leaving the starting block of a 40-yard dash. Brent is ready. He receives the baseball from Reese and throws a perfect strike to Hector at second base, just in time to catch the runner stealing, for the first out of the inning.

"Knew you could do it, Bro!" yells Jerald, basking in the glory of his correct prognostication.

Reese hits the next batter with a change-up on a no-ball two-strike count, to the dismay of the Eagles dugout and fans. Groans reverberate all around the baseball complex. The batter takes his place at first. Reese chokes back tears.

He is clearly shaken by his pitching mistake. Reese gets the next Warriors batter to hit a squirrely ground ball with tons of spin on it to KC at shortstop. KC fumbles the ball for a moment, but is able to recover, and steps on second base for the force-out, just before the runner from first reaches the base. KC doesn't even attempt a throw to first base to try for the double play because he knows his throw will not be in time to get the runner.

Hatred sees an opportunity to force its way onto the playing field. "Obstruction! Obstruction!" yells Coach Pablo, as he rushes onto the field toward the field umpire.

"What on this heavenly earth did you see on the play at second base?" yells Coach Pablo to the field umpire.

"What?" the ump shouts back. His patience is giving out.

"I'm asking what you saw on the play at second, because I saw the runner obstruct my shortstop and we should be given credit for getting the double play. The batter should be *out!*" insists the heated Eagles coach.

"First of all, Coach, you need to call 'time' before you come running onto the field. Second, *obstruction* is the fielder blocking the runner. Third, if you think the runner is at fault, it's called *interference*, which, in my judgment, it was not! Finally, your shortstop didn't throw the ball to first, to even give me a chance to call interference. So, turn around and go back to your dugout and take a seat on that silly little ball bucket you like to perch on!" the field umpire commands.

Pablo tries a new tactic. "Would you be willing to ask for help from the home plate umpire?"

"NO!!!" scolds the field ump loudly. Pablo starts walking towards home plate to ask a question. "Stop right there! It's his call, and you need to go *back* to your ball bucket right NOW!" yells the plate umpire.

Boos echo around the home side of the Field 5 stands at Lewis and Clark ballpark.

After the coach versus umpire melee sub-
sides, Reese seems to have regained control of
his emotions. The manager umpire confab has
settled Reese's nerves, and the Eagles pitcher
proceeds to strike out the final batter in the top
of the fourth inning on three straight fastballs.

Teams	1	2	3	4	5	6
WARRIORS	1	0	0	0		
EAGLES	1	0	0			

Donnie leads off the bottom of the fourth inning for the Eagles. Feeling great about finally
getting a chance to play, the determined youngster hits a shot into right field for a base hit.

"Told you, dear, that new $400 Easton Mako
bat I bought for the lad would work splendidly,"
says Donnie's dad smugly to his distracted wife
in the stands.

"Now, batting for the Eagles—Dallas!" says
the announcer, resting back in his chair.

Dallas gets the bunt sign from Coach Pablo
and lays down a perfect sacrifice bunt to move

Donnie over to second base. Dallas makes the first out of the inning, and is greeted with chest and fist bumps upon his arrival back to the Eagles dugout.

Joey stands in the batter's box, next for the Eagles. The very first pitch he sees, he awkwardly swings at, and weakly pops up the ball into foul territory very near third base for the second out of the inning.

Hector is next at bat for the Eagles. He is very patient in the batter's box. He doesn't swing at any pitches that aren't right down the middle. "I don't get up very often, so I'm making this *count*," Hector says to himself. He draws a walk on five pitches to put runners at first and second base, with two outs in the inning.

Next, the leadoff hitter for the Eagles approaches the plate. "Come on, Brentster, get a hit!" yells Brent's mom. Brent can feel the pressure of the moment. However, he's been in this situation many times during the season. The game is on the line, and his team is in need of a hit.

"Deep breath, focus, and swing as hard as you can. You got this," he encourages himself.

The first pitch is a fastball low and inside, near his knees. Brent sees the pitch perfectly, and it looks like the size of a basketball coming toward him. He pulls his hands inside of the pitch and crushes the ball over the Warriors' leaping shortstop, well into the gap between left and center field.

Donnie easily trots home with the go-ahead run for the Eagles. The Eastside Eagles dugout is a zoo. Twelve-year-old boys are jumping around like playful monkeys. Hooting and hollering can be heard for miles. Pure pandemonium ensues in the Eagles dugout.

The joyful ruckus is quickly silenced as Reese, the next batter for the Eagles, strikes out on three pitches to end the scoring threat. With his head down and tears welling up, Reese heads back to the shocked dugout as the fourth inning comes to a close.

Teams	1	2	3	4	5	6
WARRIORS	1	0	0	0		
EAGLES	1	0	0	1		

Eagles players frantically look for their gloves and hats before taking their defensive positions in the field. Keystone Cops bumping into each other have appeared more organized.

"Coach, my arm hurts," says Reese. He is rubbing his right elbow.

"Are you sure it's your arm, and you're not just sad that you struck out?" asks Coach Pablo.

Shocked and dismayed at the coach's statement, the blubbering 12-year-old responds, "No, no, it hurts, Coach."

Coach Pablo quickly formulates a strategic plan to overcome the sudden loss of his pitcher. "Mitchell, you are back in the game for Reese. Run out to first base! Donnie, hurry up and go to the pitcher's mound!" he yells impatiently.

The home plate umpire does not give Donnie extra pitches because of the injury to Reese.

"One more warmup pitch," Donnie hears from the stoic home plate umpire. Donnie feverishly wrestles with the butterflies in his stomach. He looks nervously in the direction of where his parents should be seated in the stands, but can't locate his mom or dad. He looks twice more, but cannot find a familiar face to bring relief to his frayed psyche.

"Donnie, let's go! Strike these guys out," urges Hector, as he hands him the ball after getting the throw down to second from Brent to finish the between-inning warmup sequence.

Donnie must face the top of the Warriors batting order: Butler, Gannon, and Kylan, the three hottest hitters for Westside. Donnie's first two pitches against Butler are called strikes on the outside corner. Butler fouls off the next two pitches. The count on the batter is two balls and two strikes. Donnie unfurls a beautiful knuckleball that drops out of the sky like a meteor—right into the middle of the strike zone.

"Ball," says the home plate umpire. Brent leaves the ball in his catcher's glove for ten more seconds, hoping the umpire will change his call. "Throw the ball back to the pitcher, Catch, I called it a ball!" the umpire instructs Brent.

Mothers, fathers, babies, players, and dogs around the park howl in disbelief. Donnie is dumbfounded. "Where did that miss, BLUE!" wails Donnie toward home plate.

Brent finally throws the baseball back to Donnie. Donnie takes the ball out of his glove, rubs it up a little bit, and then gets back on the pitching rubber. He doesn't get the next pitch back from the catcher. Unfortunately, Butler deposits Donnie's very next offering 250 feet away from home plate over the fence in dead center field, tying the ball game at two apiece. Deafening silence invades the third base side of Field 5 where the Eagles reside.

The pandemonium pendulum now swings over to the first base side of Field 5 where the Warriors are camped out. Spectators in center field throw the ball back into the field play, and Danny throws the ball into the Warriors' dugout for Butler to keep as a trophy.

Eagles players are shell-shocked. "Brent, son, call 'time' and go out to the mound, and tell Donnie to *flush it*—forget about it. Get the next batter," pleads his dad, hunched over on his ball bucket.

"Now batting for Westside, the Number 2 hitter in the lineup, Gannon!" comes the announcement over the booming loud speakers at the Lewis and Clark Baseball Complex. Donnie receives a brand new Little League baseball from the home plate umpire. He gathers himself and throws a pitch right down the middle of the strike zone. Gannon is ready for the pitch. He sends the brand spanking new baseball out to left field 199 feet up into the light blue Idaho sky. Dallas races from his position in shallow left field to the warning track to make an incredible two-handed lunging catch.

After the batted ball is miraculously caught in left field, Gannon takes off his batting helmet and slams it into the ground in full-throated disgust. The shiny silver metallic helmet immediately boomerangs back into his face, knocking out his two front teeth. Blood and tears streaming down his face, he limps back to the Westside Warriors dugout along the first base line. Embarrassed and sore, Gannon remains in the Championship game.

"You better be nice the rest of the year, Gannon, so Santa Claus will bring you your two front teeth for Christmas!" hollers Jerald from the Eagles dugout along the third base line. Eagles fans, having just celebrated Dallas's catch in left field, laugh uncontrollably at Jerald's insult of Gannon.

The Warriors fans respond, protesting Jerald making fun of their superstar player.

Anger boils all around the ballpark. The Lewis and Clark Baseball Complex President has his phone at the ready to speed dial the sheriff.

"Okay. Settle down, everyone. Now batting for the Westside, the Number 3 batter, Kylan!" nervously comes over the loud speakers.

Kylan steps up to the plate, and with one foot out of the batter's box, looks into the stands to see his mom pointing her finger at him with a throat slash sign. "You kill this pitcher," is the message from mom. Having witnessed his last two fastballs traveling a combined 349 feet, Donnie decides to start Kylan off with a knuckleball.

"NO!" yells Brent from behind the plate, as Donnie shakes off his sign calling for a fastball.

"YETH!" yells Gannon with his new lisp from the Warrior dugout, as he sees the knuckleball approach home plate for Kylan to swing at.

Kylan hits Donnie's knuckleball over the right field fence to give the Warriors the lead in the Championship game. He rounds third base, giving his coach a high five. Donnie is bent over at the waist, tears streaming down his face.

"Oh, dear, anyone but Kylan," says Brent's mom, an archrival of Kylan's mom Bernice. She is talking out loud to herself.

"Time, Blue!" Coach Pablo sheepishly calls to the home plate umpire.

Coach Pablo leaves the comfort of his padded ball bucket and makes the long slow slog to the pitcher's mound. Coach Pablo's eyes are firmly focused on the ground. Donnie sees the coach coming toward him and drops his eyes, as well. Brent follows his dad to the mound. Both coach and player have nothing to say to each other. "Coach, who's next?" says Brent. No verbal communication from the Coach. "*Dad!* We're still in this thing. Who. Do. You. Want. To. Pitch. Next!" says Brent in the most forceful voice he can muster.

Pablo doesn't say a word. Coach takes the new baseball that the umpire gave Donnie after Kylan's home run, and points toward the outfield with his right index finger. Coach wants Joey. Joey trots in from his right fielder position to replace Donnie on the mound. Brent greets Joey's arrival to the bump, "Let's do this thing! Get these two guys out, and we get to go hit!"

Joey delivers for the Eastside Eagles, and gets the next two Warriors batters to ground out, ending the top of the fifth inning.

"See, I told you so! If Joey was allowed to pitch, we would still be winning this game!" boasts Joey's dad two rows in front of Donnie's mom, Megyn, who is still furious that her son gave up two home runs to the Warriors.

Teams	1	2	3	4	5	6
WARRIORS	1	0	0	0	2	
EAGLES	1	0	0	1		

Coach Pablo can sense the Eagles need a spark to get the lead back to start the bottom of the fifth inning, and Danny leading off is just what the team needs to start a rally. "Danny, you made a great catch to save us in the top of the inning. Now, go find a way to get on base to start the bottom of the inning for us," he says, hoping his encouragement will change the tide for the Eagles and add to the score.

The Westside Warriors manager also senses the importance of the fifth inning. He decides now is the time to change pitchers. He brings in his best pitcher and builds upon the momentum of the go-ahead home run from his best player. Kylan struts to the pitcher's mound. He finishes his warmup pitches, then walks around the mound like a proud peacock with its wings in full display.

"Anyone but Kylan," Kay murmurs under her breath. She is repeating herself.

Danny steps into the batter's box for the Eagles, and promptly strikes out on three pitches from Kylan, two of which are wicked curveballs.

"Coming to the plate for the Eagles is the Number 4 hitter, KC!" says the announcer over the loud speakers.

Kylan glares at his catcher, Gannon, for which pitch to throw to KC. Gannon asks for a fastball. Kylan nods his head north and south in agreement.

Hatred does a fly-by over the pitcher's mound. Kylan winks at Gannon just over the top of his glove.

"Ouch! Right on my ankle! NOT AGAIN!" screams KC, as he is hit by the pitch for the second time in the Championship game. Nevertheless, KC hobbles down to first base. He knows the routine. It's the tenth time this season he's gotten hit by the pitcher with the baseball.

The Eagles fans rise to their feet, not to protest the stricken batter, but in hopes the wounded player will be able to score the tying run.

Todd is the next Eagles batter to try his luck against Kylan. The Number 5 batter is flashed the "take" sign from Coach Pablo at the third base coach's box.

"Remember, 'take' sign from Coach means don't swing at the ball, no matter where it's thrown!" remembers Todd, hitting himself in the batting helmet to reinforce the message.

Everyone in the ball park is expecting a bunt; but, instead, Todd takes the pitch for 'ball one.'

KC, however, also had seen the sign from Coach Pablo in the third base coach's box, and he sprints toward second base.

"Heeee's SAFE!" hollers the field umpire.

KC steals second base! KC is not as hurt from the hit by the pitch as the crowd thinks he was. The stolen base has visibly shaken Kylan. Kylan struggles to find the strike zone, and walks Todd on three more wild pitches.

"Turtle, that's two bases on balls today. Way to go, kid, he doesn't want to pitch to you!" yells Brent to Todd.

KC is on second base, and Todd is on first base for the surging Eagles.

"Keep it going, Donnie!" yells Jerald from inside the Eagles dugout to Donnie slowly approaching home plate.

The Westside Warriors manager just knows Coach Pablo is going to have Donnie bunt the baseball, so he instructs his third baseman to get very close to home plate.

Before stepping into the batter's box, Donnie checks with Coach Pablo for a sign. Donnie sees the sign perfectly, and understands what he must do for the team. He takes the first pitch thrown by Kylan for a ball, and the play is a double steal! KC steals third base and Todd the Turtle steals second with no throw from Gannon. Eagles runners are now on second base and third base, with only one out in the inning. KC, the tying run, is sixty feet away on third base. Todd, the go-ahead run, is on second base.

"Time!" yells the Warriors manager as he marches toward the mound.

"Listen here, you *little* superstar. Can you throw strikes? Does your private pitching coach allow you to throw strikes? Will *you please* show us how great *you think* you are and throw some strikes!" bellows the overweight Warriors manager to his star pitcher. Kylan grits his teeth and throws three straight curveballs to strike out Donnie. Donnie didn't swing at any of Kylan's pitches; the bat rested undisturbed on his shoulder.

With two down in the inning for the Eagles, Dallas is the next player up to bat. "He's thrown three straight curveballs to Donnie. I bet he's going to try another one on me," thinks Dallas. Oh, how right he is. Dallas swings. WHACK! The ball screams toward the right field fence.

"If that ball is high enough, it's going to be a home run!" yells Coach Pablo.

All fans in the stands immediately jump to their feet. As they rise like a spectacular sunrise on a spring morning, they see the Warrior's right fielder stick out his glove as he dives toward the fence and snags an incredible catch for the third out of the inning! Like a brightly colored hot air balloon being deflated, so are the Eagles players and fans at the end of the fifth inning.

Teams	1	2	3	4	5	6
WARRIORS	1	0	0	0	2	
EAGLES	1	0	0	1	0	

"Okay, guys, let's hold them. Three outs and we get to hit again. *Defense* on *three:* One, two, three, DEFENSE!" yell the Eastside Eagles. They race toward the diamond for the sixth inning.

The first batter up for the Warriors hits a line drive off Todd's glove at third base, which also glances off his chin. The ball bounces off his face to his left. He then picks up the ball and throws a rocket to Mitchell at first base. The baseball tails a little bit in flight to the right, and squirts off Milkshake's first baseman's glove, heading towards foul territory along the first base line.

The Warriors batter who hit the ball off Todd's glove, having touched first base, now quickly sees the ball getting away from Mitchell at first base. He turns from first and heads for second base. The Warriors fans, packed along the first base foul line like sardines in a can, expect their first batter in the sixth inning to easily reach second base for a clutch rally starter.

"We needed that third baseman to throw the ball away. What a great chance to get an insurance run!" chuckle two Warriors fans to each other. But the play is not over yet.

"Brent's got the ball!" screams a euphoric Jerald from the dugout. Brent has been coached all year on a ground ball hit in the infield with no one on base to trail behind the batter as he runs toward first base, just in case an Eagles infield has an errant throw to first base. Brent remembers his coaching, and bolts from his catcher's position to help his teammates. Brent trails the Warriors runner down the first base line.

Before the Warriors runner, first base coach, or fans see what Brent is up too, he picks up the overthrown ball before it goes out of play and hurls it to KC the shortstop covering second base who applies the clean tag on the Warrior runner.

"The runner is OUT!" yells the field umpire with his clinched right hand held high in the air.

The first out of the inning is recorded in the official scorebook 5-3-2-6, indicating third baseman to first baseman to catcher to shortstop.

The Eagles dugout goes nuts. Everyone is jumping up and down in full celebration mode.

"That's my baby!" says Brent's mom, Kay, clapping and staring over at Kylan's mom in the opposite bleachers.

Eagles' center fielder, Danny, makes a diving catch on a hard hit ball, and Dallas grabs a
lazy fly ball off another Warriors batter, to end
the top of the sixth inning.

Teams	1	2	3	4	5	6
WARRIORS	1	0	0	0	2	0
EAGLES	1	0	0	1	0	

Brent and the rest of the Eagles desperately
need one run to tie the Championship ballgame,
and two runs to win it. Dreams of playing on
television swirl around in all the Eagles players'
heads.

Needing one run to tie the ballgame and
send it into extra innings, or two runs to win the
game outright, the Eastside Eagles send Joey,
Hector, and Brent to face Kylan and the rest of
the Warriors team, ready to start the bottom of
the sixth and final inning.

"Folks, thanks for coming out to Lewis and
Clark Baseball Complex today. What a great
day for baseball! Please make sure to visit the
concession stands, as we've got pickled pigs feet,

four for a dollar," says the game announcer to the sellout crowd prior to the sixth inning.

The bottom of the sixth inning is "show time" for hatred and anger.

"Well, back to the action. Now, batting for Eastside, it's JOSEY!" the announcer says, loud and clear.

Joey's parents look at each other in horror. A few snickers are heard from the crowd. "It's JOEY!" his outraged parents yell from the bleachers.

Joey has one foot in the batter's box and one foot out of the batter's box, looking down at Coach Pablo for the sign.

Coach Pablo thinks to himself, *"Bunt for a base hit. Joey is fast. It's a big risk, but a big reward."* Joey sees the 'bunt for a base hit' sign from Coach Pablo, and he steps up to the plate. Joey waits until the last possible second and drops his bat down at a perfect angle, making contact to bunt the ball down toward the third base line. On contact, with the bat and ball collision, Joey takes off, sprinting for the first base bag. The Warriors third baseman picks up the bunted baseball with his bare hand and slings it toward the Warriors first baseman.

The Warriors first baseman is standing directly in front of first base, right in the base path, as Joey and the ball thrown from the third baseman arrive together like a car crash at a busy street intersection. Joey barrel rolls into the first baseman.

The field umpire yells, "He's OUT!"

The Warriors first baseman and Joey are both sprawled out, face down on the first base bag. Small drips of blood from the Warriors first baseman's jaw appear on Joey's batting helmet.

Both dugouts empty out players and coaches, like shoppers battling for super saver specials at Walmart on Black Friday after Thanksgiving Day.

The sellout crowd has gone berserk, reacting to the field umpire's "out" call, and the two ball players lying face down in the dirt.

Much like ringing the bell to start a boxing match in Las Vegas, Nevada, an empty beer can flies in from beyond the outfield fence, signaling the start of the baseball fight.

"It's alright, my precious little buddy boo, you did the right thing standing in front of first base! It was the Eagles base runner that is at fault. You didn't do anything wrong, my precious little buddy boo!" yells the mother of the Warriors first baseman from the first base bleachers to her son sprawled out face down on the infield.

Joey's mom is sobbing uncontrollably in disbelief that her son was called out on the play at first.

Donnie's mom, Megyn, has heard enough from the Westside Warriors first baseman's mom. "I warned her before the game, that if I heard that 'little buddy boo' garbage today, I was going to do something about it," says Megyn to her husband, Donnie's dad.

Megyn angrily gets up from her portable cushion-backed seat in the bleachers, and storms down three flights of steps, bumping into Joey's dad on purpose along the journey. When she reaches the ground, she flexes her left hand and rolls her neck around in four very large circles. Obviously loosening up her muscles, she strides toward the Warriors fans seated along the first base bleachers.

Standing over the top the Warriors first baseman's mom seated in the front row of the team's bleachers, Megyn shouts, "I have had enough of your 'little buddy boo' whining!" and she hauls off and slugs the mom, right in the mouth, with her left fist.

The wedding ring on Megyn's left hand cuts the mom's chin wide open, like a hot knife going through butter. Blood gushes all over her **#1 Warrior Fan & My Son Is An All-Star And Yours Is Not** tank top. The cement beneath the two women turns red in a hurry.

Joey and the Warriors first baseman regain consciousness. Both their managers are standing over the top of them, and are shouting at both umpires.

"He's safe! The first baseman blocked the base!" yells Coach Pablo.

"Your player tried to kill my kid!" yells the Warriors manager.

"Obstruction!" "Interference!" "He's out!" "He's safe!" Words fly in all directions from both managers.

The two volunteer umpires each hold up their hands toward the coaches and sellout crowd, motioning for them all to be quiet.

The first base bleachers are a scrum of adults thrashing around with some trying to fight and some trying to keep people from fighting. The third base bleachers empty out parents, like a breaking dam on the Snake River. Adults come running in from the outfield and along the foul lines to get into the fighting action.

"Call Sheriff!" hollers the Lewis and Clark Baseball Complex President into his iPhone.

"County Sheriff," answers a calm voice on the other side of the phone call. "What can I do for you?"

The President doesn't have the same sense of calmness. "Sheriff! You better send some patrol cars out to the ball diamond! We've got us a major league brouhaha!" he pleads. The two volunteer umpires are helpless in the face of the rowdy crowd and managers.

Meanwhile, anger and hatred are basking in the glow of their destruction.

Brent is on the field next to Joey, checking to see if his teammate is okay. "Joey, you good?" he asks.

"Yeah, I'm fine, Bro. Did you get the name and number on that NASCAR driver that ran me over, man?" replies Joey. He still has his sense of humor.

"More like a brick wall, dude. You should see the other guy—he's bloodied up pretty good. Let's get you back to the dugout," suggests Brent, taking charge.

Brent helps Joey to his feet and peeks over at his dad and the Warrior manager. They are screaming at each other. Pure primal rage from the two volunteer adult managers, Brent has seen and felt that anger before, from his dad, when he has failed on the baseball field.

"Get on that audio public address system and tell the crowd to stop fighting!" orders the home plate umpire to the Lewis and Clark Baseball Complex President. "We can't have moms fighting, and beer cans being thrown onto a Little League field, for goodness' sakes. Don't these parents know there are kids all around, and the curse words they are using are *obscene?* Get control over the situation!"

The President turns on the microphone and tries to calm the commotion. "Players, head back to your dugouts. Managers, go back to your ball buckets. Everyone around the ball park, please take a seat!"

The sellout crowd remains defiant, and will not settle down. Tempers are running red-hot around the ball park.

"The sheriff is on his way, and anyone that is standing up yelling when he and his deputies arrive at the field will be taken to jail for disorderly conduct. You'll spend the rest of the weekend in a jail cell," the President warns, beginning to feel a bit calmer.

Players on both teams scatter back to the dugout, like dogs trying to run on ice. Fans all around the ballpark immediately shut their mouths, and jump at spots to sit down, faster than playing a game of musical chairs.

An eerie quiet falls over Field 5, not felt since before the patrons arrived early this morning.

Warrior players return to their positions in the field. Eagles' players prepare to bat.

Order is quickly restored to Field 5. Right on time, the sheriff and three of his deputies arrive at the complex. Megyn is put in handcuffs, and is stuffed into the back of one of the police cars for assaulting another mom. The beer can thrower is identified as the owner of the Chevy Luv pickup truck, and as a pre-game heckler of the umpires. He's given a ticket for littering, and is arrested for being drunk in public. The rest of the patrons get back to their seats as fast as they can.

Hatred and anger have caused tremendous damage at the Championship game. And their playing time is not done yet.

"Alright everyone, we've got one 'out,' and a 0-0 count on the batter," the home plate ump begins, once again taking control.

Hector is the next Eagle to bat. He can barely step into the batter's box, as his legs are shaking uncontrollably from the nervous situation of the crowd and game. Like a deer in the headlights of an oncoming truck, Hector is motionless and does not swing at any of the six pitches he faces.

Hector strikes out looking, with the bat squarely on his shoulder, for the second out of the sixth inning.

"*Time!*" Coach Pablo yells to the umpire.

"Brent, come here, son. Look, the game is on the line and you've got to get a hit. The team needs you. Your mom needs you. *I* need you to get a hit. In order to play on ESPN, you must hit the ball over the fence! All the practice, since you were two years old, has been leading up to this moment. You must get a HIT!" a steely-eyed dad and coach of Brent instructs his Number 1 batter and starting catcher.

"Don't do what you did last time we played these guys in the regular season! Swing the bat and pound the ball over the fence!" begs his dad, talking directly into Brent's left side batting helmet ear hole.

Brent leaves the nerve-wracking meeting with his father in front of the third base coach's box, and makes eye contact with Kay, his mom, team scorekeeper, and his Number One fan.

Kay yells, "Have fun, Brent'er, you can do it for *all* of EASTSIDE!"

Brent approaches home plate through a fog of emotions. He begins to take a deep breath, and starts his pre-hitting routine of tapping his cleats with his bat, adjusting his batting gloves, and straightening his batting helmet.

However, this time in the batter's box, Brent can't move. He's stuck in a trance.

"What's going on—I'm a statue!" screams Brent's inside voice. He's seen the Greek mythology monster Medusa and he has turned to stone! *"Move Brent, move! Oh snap, I'm in quicksand! Help!"* Brent's brain yells to his feet. His brain frantically tries to figure out what is going on. The brain begins to send out scouts to Brent's body to find out what the heck is going on. *"We were not bitten by a rattlesnake,"* reports one of the thousand nerve scouts. *"Not a heart attack!"* reports a blood vessel scout. *"It's not an asthma outbreak!"* reports one of the

lungs. Brent's brain processes the scout's information and remains puzzled.

*What could be happening in the batter's
box? What trauma led to this kind of overwhelming paralysis?* Brent's brain focuses on
reason, analytics, and a matter-of-fact process-
ing of the reported condition from the scouts.

The brain's roadmap for where he got stuck is in
shambles. The brain takes a detour from trying
to figure out why Brent can't move in the batter's box, and looks for emotional answers.

A small voice deep inside of Brent whispers
a single word. *"Anger."*

"What was that sound?" Brent thinks to
himself. The voice continues, *"All this anger and
all this hatred at a baseball game..."* *"Who is
this?"* thinks Brent to himself.

"PLAY!" yells the umpire to the pitcher as
Brent is standing in the right-handed batter's
box at home plate.

*"Coaches are angry at coaches. Umpires are
angry at coaches. Parents are angry at parents.
Parents are angry at their kids. Kids are angry*

at their parents. Kids are angry at the umpires. Fans are angry at umpires," continues the little voice.

"STRIKE ONE!" yells the home plate umpire.

"Everyone hates everyone. No one likes each other. No one cheers for one another. There is no fun in the game. They all want to kill each other. I don't get it. Everyone treats the game as if it's life or death. So much hatred," continues the little voice.

"STRIKE TWO!" yells the home plate umpire.

The roar of the bleachers and all inhabitants of Field 5 at the Lewis and Clark Baseball Complex are in fever pitch with each side hanging onto every pitch. The noise reaches 100 decibel level, similar to an F-15 air force fight jet, taking off down the runway, heading into battle.

Brent can't shake the little voice inside him. He hears every syllable clearly. He's focused like a laser on the feelings of anger at this baseball game. Anger at every baseball game he has ever played! Not to mention all the anger on the car ride home, anger in the stands, and anger in his own heart.

Brent is caught up in his thoughts about why there is so much anger at the field. He can barely focus. The white noise around him bounces from one ear to the other. He's not sure what's going on, but something inside him is screaming for him to call 'time,' and get *out* of the batter's box before Kylan throws the next pitch.

"Uh, time, Blue?" Brent sheepishly asks the home plate umpire.

"We've got TIME!" yells the plate umpire.

Brent tries desperately to regain his composure. "Hey, Blue, what's the count?" asks Brent with his right hand wrapped in a batting glove still in the air, the signal for time.

"Batter, the count is zero balls and two strikes."

"WHAT! How the heck did that happen!" Brent angrily screams at himself. *"Wait a minute! The entire team, fans, parents, and a chance to play on television, is all on MY shoul-*

ders. I've practiced since I was two years old for this moment!" he anxiously tells himself. He goes through his pre-batting routine of fixing his batting gloves, tapping his cleats with his bat, and adjusting his batting helmet again.

With a growl on his face, Brent confidently jumps back into the batter's box with both feet. His right foot begins to dig a hole in the batter's box to gain extra traction to swing as a hard as he can. He talks back to himself. *"This is ridiculous. What have I been thinking about anger for? It's part of who I am. It's part of baseball. I will always be angry. My mom and dad will always be angry with me. Coaches are never going to like each other. Umpires will never receive forgiveness from fans, coaches, or players,"* says Brent to himself.

Kylan throws a curveball low and outside, for 'ball one.'

"Get over it," Brent commands the voices inside himself.

Kylan throws another curveball low and outside, for 'ball two.'

"Go do your job. You don't have time to solve anger issues. And I can't solve everyone else's anger and hatred issues," Brent lectures himself. He steps out of the batter's box between pitches and can see Kylan's mom Bernice and his mom Kay glaring at each other while pointing their middle fingers at each other from across the diamond.

"There is way too much anger and hatred," says the little voice inside, growing stronger.

"Ball Three!" yells the umpire.

Kylan's fastball has missed the outside corner of home plate for ball three.

"You are insane! That was strike three, you loser!" yells Kylan's mom, with a vein popping out of her sunburned neck.

The count on Brent has gone full, three balls and two strikes, with two outs in the bottom of the sixth inning of the Championship game.

Rattled by his mother's yelling from the stands, Kylan steps off the mound and looks around the entire ballpark. He fights back nervous tears that are building up like melting mountain snow behind a storage water dam.

"Why does my mom get so mad at the umpires when I pitch?" Kylan asks himself. Kylan places his right foot on the pitching rubber, grips the baseball with his usual curveball delivery, and fires the ball toward his catcher.

Kylan versus Brent, Westside Warriors versus Eastside Eagles, Bernice versus Kay—all are on the line.

"Forgiveness beats anger and hatred every single time, Brent," says the voice inside.

Kylan's curveball doesn't have much break or speed on it, and the ball bounces in the middle of home plate.

"Really? Anger always loses to forgiveness? Forgiveness always wins?" Brent questions the little voice.

"STRIKE THREE!" thunders the umpire.

Pure joy and excitement rain down on the Warrior players, like confetti coming down after a politician speaks at a big rally. The Westside

175

Warriors storm Field 5 at the Lewis and Clark Complex, in celebration that they have *won* the Championship game 3 to 2, and are headed for a date with *ESPN*!

Shock and awe cover the Eastside Eagles' side of the stadium.

Brent's face is a mixture sweat, smudged eye black, and caked-on red diamond dust clay infield—all frozen in disbelief.

Head hanging low, with chin firmly pressed against his chest, Brent is stunned that the Championship game and season are over.

"Not again," moans Brent to himself. He shakes his head and walks back to the dugout.

Teams	1	2	3	4	5	6	Final Score
WARRIORS	1	0	0	0	2	0	3
EAGLES	1	0	0	1	0	0	2

Chapter 7

Instant Replay

"Congratulations to the Westside Warriors 12-year-old team on winning the State of Idaho Little League Championship! These youngsters have earned the right to play on ESPN for the Northwest Regional Championship. We wish them the best of luck!" exclaims the game announcer over the crackling loud speakers.

The Eastside Eagles Little League players, mesmerized like moths attracted to a flaming light, stare up in disbelief at the final score blazing in neon yellow lettering on the outfield scoreboard: **3 – 2 Westside Wins** with a message that reads,

"Congrats, Warriors!"

The painful look of the 12-year-old Eagles players wiping away tears is a tough mental picture that's impossible to ignore. Spectators are still loitering around Field 5, watching the young players cry as their television and Championship dreams come down like springtime rain.

Losing the Championship game is tough. Not being able to play on television is difficult to move past for the Eagles players.

The longer the players stare at the scoreboard, the more it begins to sink in and become reality that the game and their baseball season are over. The players will cry from the disappointment of the game and letting down their parents, teammates, and coaches.

Parents and coaches will begin the post mortem ritual of reliving each negative play during the championship contest and play the 'what if' game with themselves and their kids. The thundering sound of truck tailgates closing around Field 5 can't cover-up the second-guessing noise from parents behind the outfield fence.

"Coach Pablo doesn't like my son, or he would have pitched him today," accuses an angry Eastside parent.

"We are never playing for this clown coach again. He wouldn't know what baseball talent was if it slapped him in the face," Hector's grandpa complains, as he waits on his grandson to walk to the car.

"The umpires were horrible. They cost *us* the game. The umpires didn't want *us* to win. The sun was in *our* outfielder's eyes all game long. *We* don't practice enough hitting on this team. *Our* defense is terrible. I don't know why they work on that part of the game more often," the second-guessing hurricane onslaught howls from the Eagles faithful fans.

Replays of the Championship game will not be limited to the cleanup time at the Lewis and Clark Baseball Complex. The "what if" this and "what if" that talk will continue on the car rides home and well into the foreseeable future.

"If I could just have blocked out that voice in my head talking about anger and forgiveness, I could have gotten on base and *we would have won the Championship game,"* Brent blames himself as he replays the last pitch in head.

More venomous than a cottonmouth snake-bite is the sting from youth baseball spectators toward the coach and his son when he makes the last out of the youth baseball game. Parents have an easy scapegoat for the failure of the team over a six inning game—blame the coach and his boy for the loss.

"Both games we lost to Westside this year were because of the coach's kid," says a hurt and disappointed Eagle's parent.

Brent and the other Eastside players take ownership and blame for the loss of the Championship game. The replay button in their heads will be pushed by "helpful" parents, coaches, fans, and relatives for years and years.

An honest assessment of the Championship game reveals a well-played hard-fought game between very talented 12-year-old boys. The boys are not professional athletes, but they are hard-working, determined players.

The Eastside Eagles team could not get a clutch hit with the bases loaded. The Eagles struggled to hit the ball with any consistency during the entire game. The Eagles didn't run the bases particularly well; however, they did have several chances to score runs.

The Warriors made defensive plays throughout the game. The Warriors hit two home runs over the fence. The Warriors did enough to win the Championship game and advance to play on television. The Westside Warriors side of Field 5 is the happiest place on earth next to Disneyland.

"Everyone! Everyone! Can I get your attention, please! Hey, settle down folks! Listen up! I've got an announcement!" the coach hoarsely calls to the crowd of parents, relatives, players, and siblings.

The crowd, in its euphoric state, pays no attention to the newly crowned Idaho State Championship manager. Putting his pinkie fingers together on each side of his mouth, the coach lets out a whistle that rivals a New York City Police Officer whistle moving pedestrian traffic along Times Square. "We are headed to Gannon's house to have a swim and barbeque party to celebrate this win!" yells the manager of the Westside Warriors after his ear-piercing whistle has startled the rowdy crowd.

"It won't be a late night, because we will have practice first thing tomorrow morning. Everyone will need to be at the practice field at 8:00 a.m. tomorrow," calmly states the coach.

"Coach, tomorrow is Sunday, right?" inquires a parent whose son receives the minimum two innings of playing time in each Warriors game.

"That's right. We have a lot of work to do. We couldn't field a ground ball. We couldn't hit the ball today. Pitchers couldn't throw strikes, the outfield was awful, and we are going to spend two hours on base running and bunt coverage!" exclaims the coach.

Butler, Gannon, and Kylan look at each other with familiar grins on their faces.

"He never has been able to enjoy a win. Poor guy just keeps on grinding," laugh the three best players and best friends on the Warriors team.

The three pre-teens leave the ballpark and head toward their family vehicles. The winners come face to face with the fact that tonight's Championship celebration for them will not be a party, but only a very brief time out before baseball practice drills in the early morning. Practice time and lots of it are directly in their future.

"That home run was sick, dude. Dude, you guys won the game. I can't believe it!" says Butler's six-year-old brother to anyone that will listen.

"Dude! I can't believe it! We are going to play on ESPN! I'm going to be famous!" says the backup catcher for the Warriors.

"You know, if my grandson hadn't made that double play today, I wouldn't be able to be on TV. I know they show lots of pictures of the bleachers so I'm going to have to go and get new shoes, new clothes, and a new haircut," says a Warrior grandmother to Kylan's mom as she chases after her son. He is quickly walking toward the family minivan.

The Westside Warriors are headed to the Northwest Region Baseball Championships.

Anger, hatred, and forgiveness will also have their bags packed and ready to head to the Northwest Region Baseball Championships.

Chapter 8

Scoreboard

Sitting on his catcher's gear bag, not wanting to leave the field, Brent continues to think about the Championship game. He stares up at the scoreboard on Field 5 of the Lewis and Clark Baseball Complex. "If I could just get another chance to swing the bat," he laments to himself. Over and over again, on a continuous loop replaying in his head, are the thoughts of swinging his black and gold 30 inch Easton baseball bat *just one more time* at Kylan's weak curveball. The angry demons circle over Brent's head like vultures circling a dead carcass in the Mojave Desert.

"You let down your mom, your dad, your teammates. YOU LET DOWN ALL OF IDAHO!" scream the insults. Hatred sees blood in the water like a great white shark getting ready to feast on a seal.

"I *hate* playing baseball. I *hate* letting people down. That stupid umpire is a *joke*! The ball hit the middle of the plate, for goodness' sake. That is not a strike in this league or any other stupid baseball league!" yells Brent out loud to no one.

Forgiveness waits patiently in the dugout for its time to shine.

"I'm so mad at myself and mad at my dad I could..." Brent slams his fist into the chest protector and kicks his shin guard with a violent thwack! His Eagles teammates give Brent a wide path and walk around him, as if stepping on egg shells. No one makes direct eye contact with Brent or Coach Pablo.

For the boys on the Eastside Eagles team, 12-year-old Little League season is over. What started out in January as a dream to play on television in front of millions of fans has ended at Field 5 with a thud. The players will not be

interviewed by sports reporters. No gift bags
from Little League teams from neighboring
states. No travel to the big city. No exotic foods!
No fun adventures.

Boredom sees anger and hatred having fun,
so it takes its turn heaving insults on the losing
team. "Same old stupid community pool and
same old video games," says Jerald to
Milkshake as they head to the parking lot for
the last time this season.

Brent also leaves the baseball field for the
last time this season. He turns and stares back
at home plate and wonders what could have
been. Hundreds of people who have spent the
last two hours of their lives living and dying
with each 12-year-old pitch make their way to
their vehicles. Cars begin to file out of the Lewis
and Clark Little League Baseball Complex.
Brent stares blankly at the red car taillights as
they slowly exit the parking lot. A stream of red
images moves off into the distance.

*"All those cars with all those parents and
players talking about this game...that's a lot of
anger. That's a lot of hatred. That's a lot of second-guessing. That's a lot of 'what ifs' and that's*

a lot of 'if I could've' from those people," thinks Brent.

Anger, hatred, and boredom take a victory lap and pat each other on the back upon hearing Brent's recap of their cruel efforts.

But Forgiveness sees an opening and bolts onto the playing field.

"Wait a minute. I've got it!" Like a shooting star, Brent has an "aha" moment. "It's simple, waaayyy too simple," smiles Brent. "Milo was right. I don't need to carry this anger. I don't need to carry this hatred. If other people want to get torn up in a knot over this baseball game, then that's perfectly fine with me." Brent now is chuckling out loud.

The last couple of Warriors and Eagles' straggling spectators loitering around the ballpark look at Brent like he's crazy and has lost his mind. "That boy is not right. There was something wrong with him when he was standing in the batter's box. Now there is really something wrong with him," says an Eagles parent.

"That boy is just not right," agrees another Eagles parent. I think the pressure of losing those two games against the Warriors has turned him into a nut."

"Pam was right when she forgave her dad," Brent thinks, still mulling over all that had begun in his head while he was at bat. All at once, it makes sense. "Forgiveness!" yells Brent out loud. "That little voice in my head was right!" yells Brent to the sky. "That's the answer to all the questions in my head during the at-bat against Kylan. It really *is* that easy!" Brent realizes.

The volunteer umpires are heading to the left field outfield to change out of their umpire gear back into street clothes.

"Hey, BLUE, wait up!" yells Brent.

"Yeah, Catch?" says the umpire over his shoulder. He turns back to spot Brent running toward them.

"Hey, Ump, what's your name?" asks Brent.

"Pat Campbell," the umpire answers, wondering if he is about to hear an explosion from a frustrated loser.

"Mr. Campbell, thank you for umpiring the Championship game today," says Brent with his shoulders back and chest puffed up high.

"What?" says Umpire Campbell, surprised and relieved.

"You've got a very tough job and no one likes you. You do the best you can and you try hard. Everyone blames you for all the bad stuff that happens in the game. I just want you to know I don't blame you for our team's loss today, Mr. Campbell," says Brent.

"Thanks, Catch, that is very nice to hear. I don't get any compliments with this *volunteer* job," confesses the umpire with a slight smile.

"I bet," replies Brent.

"I'm sorry for calling you out on the ball that hit the plate. Looking back on it, that was a 'ball.' I'm sorry, kiddo," says the umpire.

Brent is amazed to hear the apology, but he has something else on his mind, something important. "I found out something today," Brent says, eager to share his discovery.

Now, the ump is really curious. "What's that, kiddo?"

"I'm not angry about the call. I'm not going to hold onto hatred and beat myself up about baseball. If other people are worked up about it, then that's *their* problem!" Brent told him. "I forgive you, Mr. Campbell. And you're a pretty funny guy behind the plate. Your jokes are silly, but they make me laugh," Brent confesses.

"That's a great way to go through life, young man. I wish more people took that approach. Sad thing about it is everyone here at the ballpark today heard and saw the same message..." says Umpire Campbell.

Brent knows just what the umpire means. "Milo and Pam in the ceremonies, right?"

"You are right," nods the umpire. "Both Milo and Pam showed how to forgive others and keep moving forward in life. Bad things are going to happen. It's how you react to them that counts,"

"Forgiveness is really about me! I forgive, and that just *wipes out* anger and hatred," says Brent.

"Thanks again, Brent. Have a great rest of the summer, and I look forward to seeing you on these ball fields next season." Umpire Campbell smiles and gives a friendly wave of his hand as he turns around to catch up with the other umpires.

"Can do!" Brent yells after him.

Feeling liberated from the burden of carrying all the anger and hatred baggage around, Brent sprints toward his mom. Kay is folding up her chair, putting away her scorebook, and visiting with a few other moms about the recently completed Championship game.

"Good to see you again. Looks like we are both going to have lots of extra time to go camping this summer," Brent's mom says glumly to another mom.

"We haven't had this much time away from baseball in four years. We'll be doing lots of camping, ourselves," replies the other.

Out of breath, Brent appears right in front of his mother. "Ma..., Ma..., Mom, MOM!" pants Brent.

"Yes, Honey, what is it?" his mom asks, turning her attention to him.

"I'm not mad at myself for striking out to end the game. I'm not mad at the umpire for making a bad call!" Brent realizes how true this is, as he proclaims it to his astonished mom.

"What?" His mom is confused, not understanding Brent's happiness. After all, he lost the game.

Brent can't contain his excitement. "And I forgive myself, Mom. I'm not carrying around any hatred about the game. I'm not carrying around *any* anger from the game. I'm FREE!" yells the excited 12-year-old boy baseball player from Idaho.

"What are you talking about? You're not mad at the umpire? You're not mad at me?"

"Absolutely not. This forgiveness thing feels great, and I feel awesome!" says Brent.

"What about your father?" his mom wants to know.

"He's next on my list!!" promises Brent.

Brent gives his mom a hug and a kiss. He turns and runs as fast as he can toward the family truck. He yells over his shoulder, "Mom, you need to forgive Bernice, Kylan's mom, for whatever happened years ago in preschool. Quit carrying that anger and hatred around. Go tell her you forgive her!"

Coach Pablo is dropping off the team's equipment bag at the League trailer.

In big bold letters across the front of the snack shack are the instructions:

"All gear must be turned back into the league upon completion of your last game."

Coach Pablo deposits the team's batting helmets, catcher's gear, practice baseballs, safety kit, and baseball bat into the league equipment trailer, as he ponders what could have been.

"If I'd just let Jerald go longer in the game on the mound. Why did I call for that bunt! I should have..." thinks Coach to himself. *"I'm just so mad at myself for not sticking to my game plan,"* he seethes.

"Dad!" yells Brent from the truck toward the equipment trailer.

"Dad, hey! Over here! Hurry up and come over here to the truck!" yells an anxious 12-year-old.

Coach Pablo slowly walks toward the family truck. Still bouncing around in his head are all the possible strategic baseball moves he should have made during the Championship game to give *his* Eagles a chance to win.

"What's up, bud? I know it was a bad call by the umpire, but with two strikes you have to swing at anything close," says Brent's coach and father. He cannot resist giving a final coaching note to his son.

"Yeah, I know. I forgave the umpire for the bad call. We're friends now. It's all good," laughs Brent.

"What do you mean you forgave him? What are you talking about? Have you gone cuckoo, you little crazy bird?" teases his dad.

"Dad, I'm not mad about striking out. I'm not angry about it. I'm not going to cry about it.

195

I'm not going to throw a fit or let it ruin the rest of my day, my summer, or the rest of the time I play *baseball!*" announces a euphoric young man.

"I'm not carrying around any more anger. I'm not mad at the umpires. I'm not angry with the fans for yelling at me for striking out. I'm not mad at them for saying I lost the game. I'm not mad at mom for yelling at me," Brent proclaims, in spite of his father's puzzled looks.

"And best of all, I'm not angry with myself," he continues, feeling great relief.

"Where did all this come from, Son?"

"Forgiveness! It is simple, but awesome!" Brent explains.

"Forgiveness, huh?" replies Pablo.

"And, Dad, best of all, I'm not mad at you," says Brent softly. "I love you, Dad," he says for the first time to his father and baseball coach since he was five years old.

"You what?" questions his father, still wondering what it is all about.

"I love you, Dad. Thank you for being my dad. Thank you for being my baseball coach. I love you, Pop," says Brent.

"I love you, too, Son. I love watching you play baseball. You are really good at it! You make plays on that field that major league baseball players don't make," says Pablo.

As his dad realizes how much he means it, he finds himself choking back tears. "I'm sorry, Brent, for yelling at you."

"It's alright, Dad, I forgive you. But you've got to use this bat I found, to forgive *your* dad," says Brent.

"What bat are you talking about, Son?"

"I found the best baseball bat, ever, *for hitting anger and hatred out of the park*—it's called a 'forgiveness bat'!" Brent reveals with excitement.

For now, the number of runs on the Championship scoreboard is not the most important thing they are thinking about.

As Brent and his father hug each other, they smile and realize there is another score that counts.

FINAL SCORE:

**Forgiveness 1
Anger & Hatred 0**

Game over.

Postscript

It's time to start scoring some positive runs and beat back the huge advantage anger has taken over forgiveness in baseball on the scoreboard of life. The first step to get anger out of baseball is take an oath or pledge. Write down on a piece of paper, verbally recite, sign and frame a Code of Conduct Pledge for both child and parent. It will score points for the forgiveness team.

Get started.

Sample player and parent pledge forms are given here if you wish to use these. Or, more importantly, create your own pledge.

Read it. Sign it. Frame it. Remember it.

PLAYER'S CODE of CONDUCT PLEDGE

I, _____,(player's name) pledge to respect myself, my parents, all coaches, the umpires, all opponents, all fans, my teammates, and the game of baseball.

I understand that my attitude is more important than wins and losses.

I understand that failure is part of baseball and I will learn from those mistakes. I will immediately look forward to the next opportunity to help the team enjoy success.

I will maintain self-control on the baseball field both in victory and defeat.

I know that coaches will instruct, discipline, support, and encourage me.

No matter which position I play in the field or in the batting lineup, I will give my best effort.

I will use my unique gifts and talents to serve others both on and off the baseball field.

I am blessed and thankful to have parents that allow me to play the game of baseball.

I love playing the game of baseball.

I will forgive myself for mistakes.

I will forgive others who are mad and angry with me.

SIGNED : (Player)

_____#____

_____(Manager)

PARENTS CODE of CONDUCT PLEDGE

I,_____,
(parent's names) pledge to respect myself, my
student-athlete, all coaches, the umpires, all opponents, all fans, and the game of baseball.

I understand in supporting my child that my
attitude is more important than wins or losses.

I understand that failure is part of baseball.
My child will make negative plays on the baseball field and will learn from those mistakes. We
will immediately look forward to the next opportunity to help the team enjoy success.

I will maintain self-control around the baseball field both in victory and defeat.

I know that coaches will instruct, discipline,
support, and encourage my child.

No matter which position my child plays in
the field or in the batting lineup, I will support
the team.

I will use my unique gifts and talents to
serve all players and parents on the team both
on and off the baseball field.

I am blessed and thankful to be able to
watch my child play the game of baseball.

SIGNED:
_____#_____
                Student/Athlete/Player

_____
       Parent(s)

About the Author

As a child, Paul Venosdel spent countless hours with his brother playing whiffle ball in the backyard. From the time he was five years old, until seventeen years of age, he enjoyed playing youth baseball in California. Being selected to All-Star teams and earning a starting position as a sophomore for varsity high school baseball rewarded his exceptional abilities as pitcher and shortstop.

Now beyond school days, as of today, he has managed 24 youth baseball teams over a nine-year period. Paul's coaching and managing has impacted players from ages 6 to 14. He has managed over 400 youth baseball games against other youth baseball coaches. He uses innovative approaches while selecting, forming, and coaching his players, including their involvement each month with community service and charitable work for others. His unusual coaching and management style has paid off with more than 60% of their games being won, along with 13 Travel

Ball, League, and Tournament Championships, the most recent one being this year, climaxing an undefeated season.

Paul says that while the game of baseball is fun to play, manage, and watch from the stands, what means the most to him is inspiring truth, confidence, and character in children's lives.

Ask him, and he will tell you, his number one priority is spending time with his family. Paul says, "Every second is valuable. It will be gone in such a short time. I enjoy going to church, family game night, bike riding, going to dollar movies, watching television, attending sporting events, going out to eat, and hundreds of other events with my wife and two boys."

Made in the USA
Columbia, SC
07 November 2018